SAT
N

Cartner is gifted, bright and reasonably mouth-watering, or so *he* says. So, why aren't women falling in piles at his feet? Or are they? Is he so obsessed with the mysterious Isabella that he doesn't notice what's going on under his nose? Or is it that he's just too worried about sex – seventeen and never been . . . – to get some sort of act together?

This is Cartner's last year at school – time is running out for an old man of seventeen. Hanging around McDonald's and talking to his Word Processor is not going to get Isabella to fancy him back. So – let's have some action.

Witty, yet sensitive, *Saturday Night* reveals a teenager's last few months at school, with all the burdens of future, family, A levels and, gulp, sex.

Hunter Davies is an author, journalist and broadcaster. He has written over thirty books, ranging from biographies of the Beatles to William Wordsworth, and he wrote the 'Father's Day' column in *Punch* for ten years. He is the author of *Flossie Teacake* stories and has also written an innovative twelve-book soap series for teenagers, S.T.A.R.S., set in a North London comprehensive. He has three children and lives in London.

+ *Plus* ▶

HUNTER DAVIES

SATURDAY NIGHT

PENGUIN BOOKS

PENGUIN BOOKS

Published by the Penguin Group
27 Wrights Lane, London w8 5TZ, England
Viking Penguin Inc., 40 West 23rd Street, New York, New York 10010, USA
Penguin Books Australia Ltd, Ringwood, Victoria, Australia
Penguin Books Canada Ltd, 2801 John Street, Markham, Ontario, Canada L3R 1B4
Penguin Books (NZ) Ltd, 182–190 Wairau Road, Auckland 10, New Zealand

Penguin Books Ltd, Registered Offices: Harmondsworth, Middlesex, England

First published by Viking Kestrel 1989
Published in Penguin Books 1990
1 3 5 7 9 10 8 6 4 2

Made and printed in Great Britain by
Richard Clay Ltd, Bungay, Suffolk
Filmset in Monophoto Sabon

Contents

Frank Herrmann

Since leaving school, Hunter Davies has had a variety of jobs, including bus conductor, hodsman, timberyard labourer, postman, journalist, broadcaster, writer and gentleman. His ambition is to be rich, famous, do something meaningful and meet Miss World. He still lives in north London with his family.

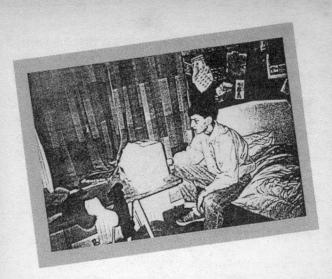

1 In Which Our Hero Says Hello, but Does Very Little

Saturday night and it's gonna be all right, tra-bloody-la. I don't think Saturday's going to be all right, or Sunday, or a week come Wednesday, or the whole boring thing I happen to have got myself caught up in at the moment, remind me what it's called, oh yeah, life. What a con. They should be prosecuted under the Trade Descriptions Act. I want my money refunded, God, old son. I think you should give people their dosh back if they're not satisfied, and I'm certainly not. Typical of these male order goods. Hey, that's not bad. Male order.

What am I doing? Stop it at once. I mustn't try to escape and fudge it and pretend and avoid the Big Issue by being silly, playing with words, playing with myself, I've done that enough recently, such as for the last seven minutes. I'm surprised I've got the strength for anything.

What am I saving myself for? Her Outside? Out there, whoever she is, wherever she is, whatever she's doing now. Ms Right, waiting at the lamppost at the corner of the universe. Or even Mrs Wrong – I'll try anything once. But who wouldn't, if they hadn't done something once? I've not been near it. But who cares? I'm getting out while the going's bad. It's not even half-time, but I want a sub brought on sharpish. Goodbye, life, it hasn't been at all nice knowing you.

Silence, but for that low fuzzy hum. PAUSE as I think about getting the car out and driving myself into a brick wall, if only I had a car, if only I could drive, if only the whole of this lousy street wasn't made of concrete. I blame that Labour council.

Quick call from God on the intercom: He says I haven't read the small print. See section five, paragraph seventeen, subsection whatsit, under no circumstances whatsoever can I exchange my life or get my money back, editor's decision final, no correspondence can be entered into with the referee. I'm seventeen and three quarters. That's what's done it. I've held on to it too long, seventeen and three-quarter weary years. If I'd let Him know earlier, He would have taken it back, no problem, we aim to please, service is our motto, biological miracles extra, see driver for details. I should have taken the anorak instead, or been a plant, or a vegetable, or a tree, or even a long-haired poodle. They were all on offer at the time, but I chose life. What a mistake.

Oh well, better make the best of it. So saying he got up off of his bed – can you have two ofs together? Why not, this is me talking to me, I can do what I like, no one else is listening, no one else is watching, no one else cares.

Oh, shurrup. I hate you when you're self-conscious. You're pathetic. You've got your arms and legs, your mind and your student bus pass, no sign of multiple sclerosis, cancer, or morning sickness, so what are you moaning on about? You jerk, you scrimshanker, wonder how you spell that, you have absolutely no right at all to lie on your bed and complain when half the population of Ethiopia can't afford a meal, and the other half can't afford to shave or buy the latest Bob Geldof CD.

Now come on, Cart, that is bad taste. Sorry. Just slipped out. It is true. I have no reason whatsoever, etc., etc. My mummy loves me. I love my daddy. My little sister hero-worships me. My teacher fancies me. I have a delightful weekend job. And best of all I'm still desperately in love with me. All's right with the world, in the best of all possible worlds, though things could be better in the League, but I think I speak for everyone assembled here in the bedroom this evening when I say good luck and best wishes to Tottenham in the New Year. Et moi.

Right, that *is* enough. You've had your whack. That's the festive season gloom over. Get hold of yourself, Cartner lad, snap out of this self-induced state of torpor, wherever that is on the map – is it near Ecuador? Search me, wish I'd dropped Geography. There I go again. Why do I do it? Don't PAUSE and think and mess around and analyse. Take life, or what's left of it, by the scruff of the neck and, and – oh, I dunno, what *do* you do with life? STOP.

That was all half an hour ago. Doesn't time go quickly when you're avoiding yourself. I've discovered a brilliant alternative to cold showers. Play with yourself. You thought I was being smutty earlier on, didn't you. Admit it. What do you think I am, an Arsenal fan? I'm referring to my new beloved instrument, my word processor. Goodness, the time has indeed flown, with not a lewd thought entering my head. Not bad for a learner, huh.

It's not actually my machine but the Old Feller's. He got it for Christmas from the Old Woman, spent three days screaming and moaning at it and now he's refusing to have

3

it anywhere near him, so it's in my room. Never thought I'd manage it, as you have to be a thicko to work all modern machinery. Only the dum-dums do computer studies, have you noticed, while the naturally gifted, such as me, do History and Geography and English, terribly hard subjects, despite being no good to man nor beastie boy. If I hadn't been so awfully clever and got all those Bs at O-level, I'd be a computer whiz by now. Remember O-levels? Sometimes, I feel prehistoric.

I've decided not to keep a diary this coming year. I think I'll remember the weather for almost every day, and what we had for supper, why write it all down, but with my new friendly WP I can avoid the boring facts and reveal my innermost boring thoughts and worries, such as 'Why is it so cold today?' and 'Oh no, not veggie rubbish for supper again.' No one will be able to read it, as the OW is in a state of collapse and the OF is stupid with all machines and can't even drive a screwdriver. He's still working out how to load the Olympus Trip he got last Christmas. It's a hanging offence if Sez even steps into my room, so she won't read it either. Perhaps even I won't. I'm bound to wipe it off by mistake. And once I get it in, then what happens? Will I ever get it out? Just like me. Ah, I feel more cheerful already. Thank you, Herr Amstrad.

I'm now sitting, reading the phone book. Some jolly good stuff in it, especially the A–D, I think that's my favourite, I just love all those dinky Deenames and pretty little numbers.

'I've done my essay, Mum, stop moaning on. You're giving me a headache.'

We have this Old Woman who lives in a shoe, somewhere down on the ground floor. (I try not to inquire too closely about the servants. Let them have their own life, I always say.) She has this thing in her head that I don't do my homework, that I sit around all day and all night in my room just

4

messing around, staring at the wallpaper, throwing darts at my vintage Glen Hoddle poster – Gawd, that dates me, almost as much as that Madonna poster that Sez has in her room. It's under her bed, hidden (so she thinks) from her friends.

I can hear two of them now in her room, or rather, I can't hear them, because her horrible loud music drowns everything. Why can't she play my sort of horrible loud music. She always turns it up to top volume the moment they come up the stairs, just to let me and them and the rest of the world know what a good time they're having. When I was fifteen, I was obscene and not heard.

'No, I can't look after her. I'm going out.'

The OW has this other thing in her head, two things in such a small head, my, my. She believes that because I'm the eldest – sorry, elder and bigger and male, or so it says on my birth certificate, another misrepresentation, I might as well be neuter for all the good my sex has done me so far – then I'm supposed to be in charge. Huh. I can't even take charge of myself. So when she and the Old Feller go out, pleasure-mad both of them, this must be the third time this decade they've gone to a party, they always say it's just in the street, won't be long, you know where we'll be, so keep an eye on Sarah, will you, till we get back.

I've been caught that way far too many times. It so happens that I'm going out tonight; well, it is Saturday, I'm not a monk, not taken any vows, even if some vows have taken me. The whole world is out, having a good time, so I'm not staying in, am I.

I can hear them now downstairs, twitting on. She'll be saying, 'That's it, we'll have to stay in.' He'll be saying, 'You never wanted to go anyway, it's just an excuse.' She'll say, 'Oh yes, blame me,' and throw something at him, then he'll take his jacket off and throw it on the floor, the bomber jacket he got in the Sixties, which he thinks makes him look young and chunky but just makes him look a right wally. I do like to hear them arguing. It makes them sort of human, don't you think. I hate polite, reasonable, silently screwed-up parents.

'Sarah, can you hear me? Turn that blessed noise down. We're now going out. I'm not sure if Cartner is staying in, but you can keep an eye on things. We won't be late.'

You would think this was Fort Knox the way they go on, worrying about their ancient Habitat furniture and stripped pine junk and amusing collections of old photies. Not as if we had the crown jewels stashed away. It's Little Sarah they're really worried about, what a laff, that some loony will come to the door when they're out and she's on her own. Any loony would run a mile. The things I could tell them.

'Look, get lost, Mum, and get out of my room, eh, stop fussing like an old hen.'

This younger generation. They frighten me, they really do, especially the female of the species. She has two friends in with her, all about seven foot high, not counting their hair. All huge and ugly, what a combination. I have to avert my eyes. The rage at this moment in time – oh, that moment's gone, the last moment then – was for fifth-formers to wear miniskirts. It's like bath-time at the Elephant House when they clump up into her room. Thighs are supposed to be sexy, so *Smash Hits* say, but this is blubber gone wild.

It's reggae music, of course, which can probably be heard on the Kingston Bypass, if not Kingston, Jamaica. When I was fifteen, I was hard and not seen.

That's the real reason I'm going out, oh yes I am, no question, out I'm going, we lepers have got to have some fun. Okay, so I'm jealous that she's got friends in and I haven't. She's got friends. In and out. So popular it makes you sick. I've got my friendly Wee Pee, but my eyes are now tiring with all the flickering. So it's Oh You Tee, out. Hello,

Saturday night. I'm not being stuck in this house on my own with those three female hooligans. Don't want to be interfered with. Well, not by them. Anyway, it's against the law. They're under age.

Now, what's her surname? Perhaps it doesn't begin with Duh. It could be foreign, but who isn't. About half of our class have names from India, China, Asia, West Indies, Greece or Cyprus ... this isn't a Geography lesson, I'm just going through our register; it's what living in London is all about, innit. One generation back, our family were Geordies and all lived in one bath, eating coal.

She only came into our sixth form last term, just one term, so short, so long, so brief, so nothing. She probably doesn't know me from Adam Ant. That's another name from the ancient past. I think my mind is fading. I did ask her to dance at the sixth-form Social before Christmas. Lol was with me, pushing me, pulling me, egging me on, saying, look out little girl, big Cartner is going to ask you to dance, it's your big night, come on you plonker, stop hiding yourself, it's your first chance for the big time. Sometimes I hate Lol.

I'd fancied her for weeks, a quiet sort of fancy, delicate and refined, which is the sort of person I am, oh yes, why be ashamed. I leave the vulgarities to Lol. He's got scores of them, you name it, he's had his hand up it, if not his leg over. Eight minutes of chat is his average, then if that fails, he's off, assaulting post-boxes or anything else that's round and shapely and offering little opposition.

And then I was sick. Right in front of her. Not my fault. Lol had said before the Social that I couldn't drink seven pints of lager. He was right. God, what an eejit.

I tried Directory Inquiries, making up the street number, guessing the spelling of her surname. I'd always thought it was Dunoon, like that town in Scotland, but nobody in the A–D with that name lived anywhere near. Perhaps it was Dha-noon, or D'Anoon, or Dunno.

'What are you doing? You've been on that phone for ages. I'm going to start charging you, Cartner, it's gone too far.'

I thought the Old Feller had gone out. What was he doing picking up the extension, listening to my intimate conversations? I could have been telling disgusting confessions to Directory Inquiries, if only the rotten lot had answered.

'I'm trying to ring Lol. He's got my essay.'

'Well, hurry up. I'm trying to book a minicab.'

'I thought you'd gone out.'

'I thought you'd gone out. If I'd known you were staying in, we could have left earlier and I wouldn't be needing to book a minicab.'

'I'd go out, if you'd get off the rotten phone.'

'Directory Inquiries,' said a tired, bad-tempered voice.

'You rotten sod, Lol,' I said. 'Where's my bleedin' essay? I just said you could look at it, not copy out the whole thing. I want it back now, toot de flaming sweet, so make it pronto . . .'

I then hung up, leaving Directory Inquiries in mid-sentence and my Dad working out what the hell was going on.

I marched down the stairs, my best determined walk. I know where I'm going, I know who's going with me, and other lies and nonsenses and pretences, fooling no one, hiding nothing.

The OF was bending down, picking up his Sixties bomber jacket. I could see his bald spot on the top of his head, about the size of a small saucer. Seems only yesterday it was postage-stamp size. And the day before yesterday Sez used to sit on his lap and brush his long, thick black hair till the OW said, that's enough now, Sarah, don't overdo it. That was in the good old innocent days, long before Child Watch. In fact I can hardly remember it. I think that little scene comes from one of his own 8 mm home movies, the silent ones, which we have to watch every New Year's Eve when the OF gets maudlin and insists we all watch and think nice family thoughts. Pass the yuck bag, Alec.

The O W was sitting on the living-room couch, looking soulful, taking off her high heels, I do not want to go out anyway, let us call it a day, you go on your own, dear, really I won't mind, go and enjoy yourself. Bloody hell. Spare me. Thank gawd I'm going out, having good times, getting away from this geriatric pantomime.

I banged the door, hard and loud, then the front gate, crash and bash. Then I stood thinking, hmm and hmm. Who was I going to honour with my company? I could have turned right and entered an exciting new stage in my life, which meant starting at the Bull and Frog, or turned left and at once I'd be over the page, sorry, on to a new disc, and meeting such fascinating people, such beautiful girls, which meant my new exciting life would be commencing at the Brookfield Arms.

I wanted to go both places, all places, go each and every way, if you don't mind, one after the other, experience each and every avenue, and then retrace and decide which I liked best. Was it Sartre or JB Priestley who did all those clever-clogs time tricks? Or HG Wells? Hold on, it's Saturday night, which means no thinking, give us a break, no in-tellectual stuff. Anyway we're doing boring old Macbeth for A-levels, and boring old Wordsworth. Now, what's our novel? Some Victorian crap. I've forgotten it already, and it's only five months till the exams.

Good job I'm young, gifted and bright. And I have bits of paper to prove it. We now have self-assessment reports at the end of every term. I wrote that I'm young, gifted and bright on every page. Old Arseface was not at all amused. Let's hope, Livingstone, that when and if you manage to secure a university admission interview, you will try to re-strain your infantile sense of humour, at least for a brief moment in time. Oh shurrup, you old twat.

I stood on my own and drank two half-pints of lager in the Bull. No sign of that beggar Lol. He promised he would be here. A fat kid called Darren I used to sit next to in primary school pinned my ear back about Spurs' off-side trap, and why it was doomed to failure. I listened politely as he now has a big gold chain round his neck, tattoos all over his massive arms, and boasted that he was running a minicab firm. I then became convinced he was going to buy me a double rum for old times' sake, remember Miss Button and that time we saw her knickers, but he suddenly announced his Roller was on a double yellow and he'd have to go, well fast, see you Cartner, keep in touch, sucker.

I moved on to the Brookfield where I had some prawn crisps, which I hate, but the barmaid said, 'Prawn crisps, son, your usual, eh?' God knows who she thought I was, and I said, yes, make it snappy, and crispy.

A girl called Tracey, who used to be three feet high with specs and braces was sitting on a bar stool, trying to look like Marilyn Monroe's sexy sister. She's just joined the Lower Sixth, but was trying hard not to show it. Resitting Domestic Science, I think, or Knitting. She gave me a smile then re-crossed her legs. The gorilla she was sitting with followed her gaze and saw it was me. He laughed. The pig. I once locked Tracey in the infants' lavs and tried to get her to take her dress off, but she pushed my head down into the water and climbed over the lav door and I was left, locked in. I was two feet high at the time and small with it. Not much has changed. No wonder I've never scored.

I used to long to be an orphan. Seemed such a mysterious, romantic thing to be, till my Dad told me he had some National Savings Certs, taken out in my name when I was born, which one day could be worth, phew, a fortune, so I decided to hang on as me. He says they will be mine if I get to twenty-one without smoking. I've offered to do without wine, if he'll double it, and women as well, for triple. No, that would be too easy. Not a test really, why take his money from him, poor old sod, he'll need it all soon to get himself a decent hairpiece.

Then I went through a stage of wanting to be a single child, not having this pesky little sister bugging me, not having to share things, consider her feelings or look after her. I tried to drown her when I was four, throw her off the swings when I was five, chuck her out the front window when I was six. Since then, she's grown rather, and all I can hit her with is sarcasm. Not that she notices much, being thick-skinned.

There was also a stage, hope you're taking notes, when I wished we'd moved around a bit more. So feeble being in the same house and the same street all one's life. The Old Folks are so proud of having given us this, continuity, stability, all that rubbish, but I'd prefer to have been a nomad, a different school every term, different friends, different personalities you can assume each time. It would be neat to have tried on another character, been able to discard my old and jaded personalities, especially the one I'm using now. I wouldn't buy this from a second-hand hair salesman. When you stay put, the rest of the world gets an image of you, rightly or wrongly, which you then become, and you get stuck with it, forced to respond to it, locked for ever in your own identity kit. You crouch inside, desperately waving, saying, hey folks, that's not really me, har har, all that horrible exterior stuff, yes I did say that, yes I did do that, but look properly, please, there's a real and lovelier me just waiting to creep out.

I suddenly remembered Isabella's second name. Dineen. Not Dunoon. Quite attractive. I do like these ethnic names. I did ask her once in the corridor if she was Spanish, which didn't get me very far. I was thinking of Isabella and Ferdinand, the Catholic monarchs, we did them at O-level. She looked at me as if I was half-witted, then turned away and went into the library. I can smell her now. The scent of her body, the fragrance of her being, the pink of her hair. I tell a lie. It was sort of just lightly bleached at the front, the fringe bit, all the rage last term. Goodness, what mad fashions will next term bring. How can I contain myself.

'Is that Mrs Dineen?'

I could hardly hear myself speak above the noise of the pub's juke-box. I shouted the name again, pronouncing it differently, just in case I'd got it wrong.

'Is Isabella there?'

This time I said each syllable separately, as is not my wont. I do tend to gabble things. In my head I'm ever so fluent, ever so smooth, ever so witty, but in the flesh, which is what I happen to be going around in at the moment until they improve polystyrene, I can be rather clumsy and mumbly and hard to understand.

'Hold on pleeze, I go get her.'

I was sweating, not like me; what a lie, it's exactly like me. I should have put my best trainers on. I'd come out in my other pair, the ones the O W has banned from the hall. One never knows in life, does one, oh belt up, no really, one should always be prepared, one's best foot forward, ready for anything that might be offered, without having to say, excuse me, dear, I cannot jump into bed with you, you know, you might not have noticed, but I've had these boxer shorts on three days, or is it three weeks, hold on a tick while I go home and change. One should be Toujours Prat, as they say in the French Boy Scouts.

I started coughing and choking. It was the smoke, of course. Being a non-smoker, I do feel it in the old lungs. And the manic whine of the video games and the fumes of the rotten gassy beer and the cheapo wine being slurped by those dying blokes at the bar made it worse. For all I know, some of those deceased might even be women, what a den of iniquity and sin have I wandered into, save me, oh save me, my own sweet Isabella, take me away from all this.

'Sorry? Can you speak up?'

A bloke's voice had now come on the line. He seemed to

be demanding who it was, but I could hardly hear a thing he was saying.

'Can I speak to Isabella?' I shouted. Too loudly, really. There was a sudden pause at the bar and they all turned round. Above my head I could see various names and numbers written on the wall in black felt pen, ring Anna for French Lesson, Moira for a Massage, Harriet for an Intimate Horoscope and Isabella for Leather Goods.

I suppose I do look like the sort of weedy little sixth-former who has to resort to such things, poor lad, doesn't know what it's for, no lead in his pencil. It'll be round the sixth form tomorrow, and our street and everyone I've ever met in my life will be pointing at me. He has to ring up call-girls. THE MAN WHO'S NEVER HAD IT AWAY.

'Oh, it's just a friend, from, er, just a friend.'

I didn't want to say school. I pulled myself up to the full five feet eight inches that I say I am, hoping perhaps that one of those dead drunks, half canned though they are, might mistake me for Sylvester Stallone or Robert Redford.

I waited. What was I going to say to her anyway? Terribly sorry, Isabella, about the Social, you know, about what happened, it's just that, well not many people know, but I've just been to South America on a Geography Field Course and I've picked up this unusual tropical bug, you know what it's like, usually I'm fine, but this time, blow me, it got to the old tum, sorry to be vulgar.

'She's not in? Oh.'

Hell. Taken them long enough to find out. Must live in an enormous house, or a hostel, or a dosser, do I want to get mixed up with such a person. I have my vows to think about.

'Hold on, sorry, you don't happen to know where's she gone, hmm?'

There was another long wait and a lot of clatter and whispering and confabbing, then the first old crone with the foreign accent came back on the phone.

'She gone out half hour go. She gone with some poison called Lol. That all she say.'

Then she hung up. Merry Christmas, Cartner old son. And all the best for the New Year. If you're going to make it. If you're going to go ahead and try it. If I were you, I'd give in. Seventeen years have been bloody useless. What chance have you in your eighteenth?

2 Some Thoughts on the English Education System

There was an intellectual conversation going on in the sixth-form Common Room. Oh, typical of our usual high-powered stuff, state of the nation, state of the art, that sort of thing. No one can say we are Common in our Room. We sixth-formers are a cut above those boring fifth and lower years. We have our own room, so it must be true. It's about the only reason people ever stay on, just to get inside the sixth-form Common Room, say they've been in, become a member, met the all-time greats, those who have been made legends in their lunch hour.

School life is in fact just the same, dreary as ever, except for our room, a place where one can cower, one can retreat to in times of stress, that's if you can fight your way through the fug and the junk and the bodies.

Someone had at least cleaned it up after the Social. It looked almost respectable, a hint of fresh air, fresh feelings, how apt for the first day of the new term of a new brave year. My last. I'll probably cry in the end. They always do.

'What's that nasty smell,' shouted someone. 'Oh no, it's Cartner.'

Naturally I ignored such primary-school remarks, gave them the cold stare they deserved, but when I sat down, I did have a quick look at my trainers. My second-best pair, almost in shreds, seen service, but I'm sure they don't smell, not very much. My best pair has disappeared. Very strange. I looked for them after I'd been to the pub, but they'd gone. The OW will go mad if I mention it. She's always moaning that I lose everything.

I realized that all the groups were for once united, joining in one fascinating topic. Usually we grind on about our own subjects in our own corners, the poseurs posing away, the haircuts admiring each other, the soul boys grooving on the windowsill, the casuals standing near the door trying to protect their creases, the feminists sitting in a circle, the druggies lying in a circle, our Asian friends reading maths cards, the heavies taking turns to try out their new boots on each other, the Sloanes having hysterics, the creeps walking in and out quickly with their files looking purposeful, the drears worrying about their spots, the intellectuals worrying about their image and their UCCA forms. All human life is there, crawling around somewhere, though an absolute stranger, popping in from Mars, would probably see it all as one large amorphous mass, wearing the same clothes, the same looks, missing completely all the tensions and tribulations that have gone into each and every offering for that first Monday morning of term. Even the drears have made some sort of decision, if only to put on what they wore yesterday and the day before.

We have an Open sixth-form, whatever that means, oh

yeah, you don't have to pass any exams, just pretend you're on some sort of recognized course that will lead to some recognized something or other, such as a City and Guilds Grass-cutting Certificate or a Cambridge entrance examination. I still don't know some of the kids, as many have arrived from different sorts of school, fed up with their previous existence, fed up with their teachers or themselves, come to try a new life. The public school drop-outs get ignored at first. I hate them, but only because they haven't put up with what we've put up with, lucky sods, five years of hell, five years of disruption. Well, perhaps it was only three years of chaos, don't want to exaggerate. I did learn a lot. Ask me anything about Inner City Social Problems. It has made me the Man I am today. I am a walking, talking, breathing advert for the Comprehensive system. You can take me anywhere and I'll fit in. Just as long as it's another Comprehensive sixth form. They tell us the real world out there will be like this, not like the playing fields of Eton. God help the real world.

'You half-witted plonker,' shouted Lol. 'Dougal was in *Trumpton*.'

'No he wasn't,' said Silas, our resident brain-box, star of stage, computer screen and all As at O-level, don't talk about him. 'He was in *The Magic Roundabout*.'

Everyone immediately joined in, trotting out their boring memories, the stories, the characters they used to watch on TV back in ye olden days, somewhere in the distant Seventies, God, I can hardly remember it myself. People were shouting all at once, do you remember *Batman*, what about *Captain Scarlet*, and that good bit in *Thunderbirds* when, and hey, who was that bloke in *Star Trek*, no, that's not the theme tune, you wally, you're getting mixed up with, no, really, my favourite was *Banana Splits*. More cheers and shouts. Even the creeps stopped walking back and forth to contribute their tiny memoirs. There was a polite pause when Clarrie, our resident Sloane, came out with her bit without anyone mocking her accent, and Tracey was allowed to speak without someone telling her to get them off.

There's nothing that unites a group more than mutual memories of what they all watched in their formative years, however they've ended up, tall and manly and super-sophisticated like me, or a nasty crude jerk like Lol. We have our past in common. And very boring it can be. I plan to leave the meal table if my Dad tells me once more about Dick Barton, Special Agent.

But this time it was interesting, thanks to Young Silas.

'I'll tell you something really fascinating,' said Silas.

'Let us be the judge of that,' said Vinny, coldly. Everyone laughed. Vinny is usually so cool that he doesn't waste a lot of time talking, he puts all his energy into how he looks.

'Okay, I won't tell you,' said Silas.

'Oh, come on, darling,' said Lol, putting on a camp voice. 'I'll be your best friend.'

'You can have a bite of my Mars Bar,' said Tracey.

'I'll take you into the next P G film,' said Clarrie.

'Tell you what,' said Lol. 'I'll go to the bogs with you, next time you have to go. Can't say fairer than that.'

'You're all so funny,' said Silas, standing up, getting his plastic bag of books ready.

'Oh, come on, Silas,' I said. 'You know you're going to tell us anyway.'

'Not now,' he said, putting on his serious, hurt expression, which made everyone laugh even more. For all his cleverness and brilliance he always found teasing hard to take. Rather reassuring, shows he's human.

'Oh, your worship,' said Lol, pretending to kiss the floor in front of him. 'Your Majesty, do bestow on us one of your little gems, give us the benefit of your wit and wisdom, yuck, your feet smell, Si, what you been doing with them?'

'Just ignore him,' said Clarrie, grabbing Silas's arm and

making him sit down. 'We really do want to hear. Don't we?'

There was a big cheer all round and people began singing and chanting. 'Come on, Silas.' 'We want to hear.' 'Why are we waiting?' 'Here we go, here we go, here we go.'

The room was in an uproar, but it was for Silas, not against him. He stood in the middle and waved his hands, smiling, waiting for everyone to calm down, but of course when these chants start, people keep them going just to keep them going, soon forgetting the point, if there ever was a point.

'Whatever I say now will be an anti-climax,' said Silas. 'You've successfully ruined it. You did it deliberately, didn't you, Lawrence?'

'What, sir? Me, Sir? Not me, Sir,' said Lol, pretending to be a first-former.

'I was only going to make a minor observation,' said Silas.

'Oooh, minor observation,' said Tracey. 'Get him.'

'Anyway,' said Silas, determined to tell us his bit of trivia, which he had been all along, as everyone knew. 'Who remembers watching *Bill and Ben*?'

Lots of people shouted and put up their hands. Most of them liars. I vaguely remembered them being talked about, but I don't recall actually watching them. My life started with the Wombles.

'You mean Bill and Ben the Flower Power Men,' said Lol.

'Ha ha,' said Silas.

'Were they in *Trumpton*?' asked Tracey, but everyone ignored her.

'*Bill and Ben, the Flowerpot Men*,' explained Silas. 'They were very popular at one time, but then they got taken off.'

Everyone waited.

'Is that it, then, Si?' said Lol. 'Really fascinating. Glad we all waited.'

'They were taken off because someone in the BBC decided they were gay.'

'Oooh, naughty,' said Tracey.

'How do you know this incredible fact?' asked Clarrie, all wide-eyed.

'My uncle, actually,' said Silas. 'He used to be an electrician at the TV Centre.'

'Oh, I see,' said Lol. 'Friends in low places.'

The bell went. Vinny and the poseurs regrouped, the soul boys got their fingers clicking in time again, the feminists linked arms and trudged out together.

So we end another play-time, another pause in life's busy round of work, work, work. All except for those maintaining they have a free period, God, look how many are staying behind, all bunking off, I bet . . .

I sat behind Isabella, the beautiful spy, breathing in her ambience, fantasizing about her underwear. No, that's not true. This is an idealized idealism, if you can have such a thing. No smutty thoughts were being allowed to enter my tired-out little mind. Let's have some purity in this wicked world. You will always be on a pedestal to me, my petal. I just love the way you are, the way you sit, you look, you stare, the way you take notes in your lovely handwriting on *The Prelude* while I sit silent, lost in rapture, lost in space. I wonder where you've come from, where you're going. Apart from Heaven. Can that be private school handwriting (looks suspicious), or is it from foreign parts? For just one term have our lives crossed, yet I have uttered just one sentence to your face, then left my visiting card on the floor in front of you. What a fool.

'Livingstone, would you be good enough to tell us why Wordsworth started writing *The Prelude* while he was in Germany?'

That was news to me for a start. I thought he wrote all

his junk while in some cottage in Grasmere, shacked up with his dopey sister and all those other weirdos, drinking porridge and eating opium.

'Does it really matter where he wrote it?' I started, muttering and mumbling. Old Barnes has always hated me, never rated me, he only has time for that creep, Silas, or the girls, so why should I knock myself out?

'Yes, that's why I'm asking you the question.'

I looked around. Most people were pretending to be really bored. Lol had a copy of 2000 AD on the table in front of him, waiting for Barnes to tell him off, which he wouldn't. Barnes was too smart for that. Vinny had both eyes closed, but then he usually did. Only the girls seemed to be paying attention. Some were even taking notes. In Barnes's lessons there was at least relative silence, with no actual disruption.

Barnes stood, tapping his stupid fingers on the desk, waiting for me.

'Well, I think it's sort of the fact he wrote it, that's what matters. We should be studying that, not worrying about where he went for his hols. I think, you know, there's too much of this going on, this bringing in biographical stuff. It's the stuff itself we should be examining, without knowing anything about the bloke what wrote it, if you ask me, and if you ask me, it's a load of cobblers anyway . . .'

'Thank you, Livingstone. A controversial contribution, as ever. Isabella, can you enlighten us, hmm?'

I hate the way Barnes always calls the boys by their surnames and the girls by their Christian names. We all know he's a Fascist beast who beats his wife and starves his kids, but he thinks he's ultra-cool and correct. Even Sal, the leader of the Slags, our resident feminist freedom-fighters, brought it up at the school council, demanding that he address all girls by their surname, but he refused. He does happen to be a pretty good teacher and my only hope for a B, if I'm lucky, and he does work hard and he gives good lessons and keeps us at it, but basically he's just a common or garden pig.

'Wordsworth found that being stuck in a remote part of Europe,' said Isabella, 'made him conscious of where he had come from, who he was. It often happens that you need to travel in foreign parts to discover your home.'

Oh God, what a swot, and what a smirk from that creep Barnes. Don't say he fancies her as well.

It's bad enough having that slob Lol hanging around, not that I'm talking to him any more, or her, not if she went out with him on Saturday. I'm not even going to ask Lol about it. That's her finished. The end, before there was even a beginning. No, it can't be true. She must have more taste than that. Not that I'll ever find out. Too late, too late, they cried in vain.

I found myself walking down the corridor beside her, don't know how, sheer chance, you know me, a man of moral principle and breakfast fibre, once I've made my mind up, well, anything at all can make me change it.

'I think you've got a point,' said Isabella.

I examined my trousers at once, then realized such third-form smirks were not called for, not in the presence of an Hintellectual Bluestocking. Yes, I can see closer now. What skin, so soft, so silk-like, I'd like to have her on my bath-rack, ready to rub all over me, her bottled, perfumed essence kept for my personal use, along with my Uncle Orinoco sponge and my Dougal shampoo-bottle, which no one is allowed to throw out, ever.

'You really think so,' I replied, all non-sha-long.

'I've thought that myself. A text should be able to stand on its own. We shouldn't need to know about the author, the poet or the novelist, him or her.'

'Too late now,' I said. 'There's a whole industry been built up round all these famous poets and that. You can get a living out of it, even a low form of living like teaching English.'

'I thought Mr Barnes was rather good today.'

'I think he's a berk.'

'Compared with the teachers we had at my other school, then he's . . .'

But she didn't finish. I was about to get some personal gen, but she'd cut herself short. One has to wait to be told. One does not ask personal questions, not in our sixth form. Parents' jobs are never inquired about. Class is not stated. Home life is not revealed. Personal predilections of a sexual nature are not commented on. They don't matter, any more than the colour of one's skin. One is. One is accepted, or not accepted, as is. Not because of where one has come from. End of statement. Boring, innit. Sometimes it drives me mad, trying to guess people's parents and their homes and their sex lives.

'I don't care for all this analysis, anyway,' I said. 'It's all phoney. I think you should just be able to say you like a poem, or not like a poem. It's no different from liking or not liking marmalade, but we have to go through all this poncing about.'

'Oh, I rather like it. It clears your head, makes you think, when you have to examine what you *do* like, and why.'

She gave me a little smile. Until that lesson, I'd been a mere speck on her horizon, one who had happened to blow across her path and to her surprise she found me, what shall we say, not totally uninteresting? Hmm. Is she at last becoming conscious of this little weedy speck in his Fred Perry pully and Marks and Spencer vintage trainers. Goodness, could he be the very same boy, I do declare, who was disgustingly sick at the Social? Don't push it, Cart. Keep opening the doors. Say nothing gross.

'Hi, Bella,' said a voice, one I know only too well. 'Are you and me gonna do some little practising this weekend, huh, honey-bunch?'

Lol has this leer which he thinks is a sending-up leer, is a taking-the-mickey-out-of leer, an assumed lecherous leer, but he's done it for so long, since he was in the first year chasing primary, prepubescent skirt, that it has now stuck on his face and just looks, frankly, well, repulsive.

Isabella smiled, the same sweet little smile she had been proffering my way. What goes? What happens? Doesn't the world see the difference?

'That would be nice.'

'Friday night, then, it's gonna be all right.'

Isabella went off for French. Me and Lol went off to the pub for a quick half before lunch, not that I wish to associate with such characters, such slobs, such pigs, but he did say he would pay.

He leered at me over his glass, meaningfully. I refused to ask him about Isabella, if he had got his end away, if she was a goer, all that stuff he was just waiting to tell me. I was no longer interested. She was a stuck-up bitch, really pretentious. I'd rather talk to Sez than her, if I was really desperate for female company, and I'd have to be. Yet if she's stuck-up, why does she go out with Lol? Perhaps she likes the occasional bit of rough trade. And they don't come rougher than our Lawrence.

'Going to Spurs Wednesday night?' I said, trying to raise the tone.

'Can't. Got an all-night gig in Hackney.'

Another subject not to ask him about. All I would get would be more boasts about his latest group and his prowess on the drums.

'In fact I'm fixed up all week. Tomorrow we're seeing this recording agent who's dead keen. Saturday, now what's Saturday? Oh yeah, Tracey's party.'

'I'll probably go to Spurs again, if I'm not working, though the way they're playing I'm surprised anyone bothers.'

'The party's in the evening, you wally. You are coming, aren't you?'

'What?'

'She's got the hots for you, gawd knows why. She asked me to make sure you come alone. So I'll come for you, about eight. Ciao.'

3 Our Hero Is Invited to an Orgy

The Old Feller asked me for a game of snooker after supper. I'm often kind that way, considerate to the poor and the deprived. I really wanted to sit and read my old Spurs programmes, which I've collected since I was seven, all neat, scores recorded, subs listed, Bovril or tea at half-time. It's the sort of thing I do when I'm feeling soulful or sorry for myself and want to dwell on times past and perhaps have a little weep about yesteryear. How is Glenn getting on these days, I wonder, sob sob. But I can't find them. They were under my bed, kept for emergencies, such as night starvation, but now they're not there. I think my memory is going now.

'Okay then, just one game, to humour you.'

He's absolutely useless, but won't admit it. The table is so lousy even I don't play to my full potential. He bought it for me for Xmas about a million years ago, when I was fourteen, a cheapo job made of hardboard, and it's now so worn it's like playing on a ploughed hillside. But he does enjoy it, poor thing. 'Father and son playing together.' I can see the quotation marks oozing out of his simple mind and hanging over his bald spot like a halo when he bends down to do a tricky shot.

We were playing for a fiver, one I owed him and had no intention of paying back anyway; what else are fathers for, he's in work, isn't he? Or so he lets us believe when he goes off every morning. His job is answering telephones. That's all he did the only time he ever dragged me and Sez to his office.

I was being fairly kind to him as I have pinched his WP, not that he seems to have realized. Just hope he doesn't want it back. The OW has also pinched his camera, another Christmas present he's never managed to work. I dunno. This older generation. Completely spoiled.

I was really killing time, waiting for two things. My old trainers for a start. That lousy OW would not let me put them in the washing machine yesterday when I went off to school, she can be so mean, said it was a waste of money putting it on for just one item. They would have been dry by now but for her. So I did them myself this morning, which is why they are still sodden, despite a couple of spins in the heat bit, which I'm not supposed to use as it's on the blink and anyway, Cartner, you should never expose shoes to any kind of artificial heat. Oh shurrup, you old bat, whose shoes are they anyway? They also happen to be the only ones I've got now.

I need them clean for tonight, don't I? I don't want to pong the place out right in the middle of an orgy. That's what Lol has promised. He goes to one every night, and twice on Saturdays. I'll be revealed as having wet feet instead of smelly feet, which I suppose is better. I could, of course, spend the evening with my trainers on, but one has to be prepared in this life for all eventualities. I might be getting my feet away tonight.

I was also waiting for Lol. He was already hours late, typical, the orgy will have orged by the time we get there. Can't go on my own as I don't know where Tracey lives. No hold on, I did go to a party of hers when I was nine. We had this kissing game with funny hats on and I tried to avoid her but failed, as she was rigging the game. Her braces drew blood from my bottom lip and they had to ring my Mum to take me home.

I often look at that old primary-school photo and ponder, peering into faces, trying to wonder what happened to all those little people, that angel Anthony, now on heroin and as good as dead, that sweet Angela last seen on the game at King's Cross, poor old Christodoulo who could speak no English and is now at Oxford. Those pretty faces, where did they all go. All the girls I wrote love letters to, whose names I scrawled in my Neat Book, who once seemed so pretty and are now squat and dreary and stupid and hoping, fingers crossed, Cartner, to work at Sainsbury's.

Tracey was considered the pits. No one would sit beside her. Amazing that she's turned out so glam, if you like that sort of peroxide glam. Personally, give me any glam, any old thing, small or big, real or bought, just make it quick.

Hmm, what about me? Hmm again. How has old Cartner changed? For the best, of course. No, let's not start that. This data disc is filling up too fast and I've only got one, which I've got to keep hiding all the time, just in case. We'll just have the fax, man, not the fantasy.

*

So I was walking at last down the street with Lol, squelching away, leaving wet prints on the pavement, no one can say I made no mark on the sands of time, let this be my memorial, wipe not this effigy away, O Camden Council.

'Oh hell, Lol, it's Camden Tube.'

I have little sense of direction, and still need chalk marks when I get up in the night to find the lav, but I could see at once where we were, the nastiest rendezvous in the Northern Hemisphere, why do we do it, haven't we all got more sense. I can never decide which turns my stomach more, the young druggies injecting themselves, the old drunkies throwing up, or just the middle-of-the-road derelicts lying among their pathetic bundles.

'Tracey doesn't live here, does she?' I said.

'Yeah, her dad's a guard and they all live with him in his cabin, up and down the Northern Line all day long, telly reception is terrible, but there's no heating bill . . .'

'Bugger off, clever clogs,' I said, not that I normally swear aloud, but I do tend to take on the colour of the slobs around me. It was a silly question, anyway. I knew only too well why Lol had dragged me here. The way to an orgy every night and twice on etc., is to be ever on the lookout for other and better orgies. Lol begins every night of his sordid life by checking into Camden Town tube, finding out where everyone is going, making mental lists of addresses and names, even following total strangers if he's stuck, so that wherever he does go off to, he can split at once if he's made a mistake, then go on to the next venue. He usually carries his drumsticks with him, pretending he's in the group, any group.

'I hear there's a good party on at Arlington House tonight,' I said. 'Just your scene. Some lovely Irish talent and all the meths you can drink.'

'Get lost, fatface,' said Lol. So we were now even.

Lol followed a few gangs, talked to some weirdos, checked

a few names, then we set off towards Mornington Crescent. I eventually did vaguely recognize Tracey's block of flats, about ten miles high, built like a prison. It didn't look too bad when I went there eight years ago, but I was young then and awfully impressionable.

I used to moan that it wasn't fair, why did we live in a house not a flat? You always have people to play with, when you live in a flat. I was quite ashamed for a while of having our own house, a crummy terrace house though it is, owned by the Halifax, falling to pieces, as it does mean, alas, that the O F is a capitalist pig, do keep it quiet or I'll have no pavement cred. But I do have my own bedroom, oh rapture. So does my pig sister.

Lol shares his with two older brothers, both dodgy minicab drivers who come in at all times of the night, no wonder Lol never goes home. No wonder he can't study. Yet he's one of the most naturally clever blokes in our year. Never does a stroke, and has no intention of ever doing so, but he can understand everything at once, while I'm still saying, hold on, sir, did you say longitude or latitude, who is this woman Lucy he's always on about, and these Stephensons, is Robert the dad or George? When I do get something into my little nut it usually stays there, sometimes for over half an hour, but it has to be explained very simply, in syllables of one word, right at the beginning.

Sez is quick. Too quick by half, if you ask me, which you didn't, unless you're wired in. Hey, that could be possible. I've heard of kids busting computer codes and robbing banks. What do you think of it so far? Cheeky. Well, if you're so clever, any idea what's going to happen tonight? No, neither have I, so get off my screen, please. Now where's the C A N for cancel? Right, that will teach you to interrupt when I'm on the job, ha ha.

Lol insisted we took the lift, which looked pretty scary, full of litter, with bits of wire hanging out, every wall covered with obscenities, most of which I totally agreed with. ARSENAL STINK. Nice to feel at home, among friends and fellow supporters. The light went off as we went up, so it was even scarier, but Big Lol would protect me if any nasty persons lunged at us when we got out.

No one did, but I got vertigo just walking along the open concrete landings. Remind me not to drink tonight, Lol, I feel dizzy just looking over the side. How did they survive this? Several Alsatians rushed at us, trying to grab our ghoolies, which I'd brought with me, just in case I might need them, but Lol kicked and swore at them and they went back to fighting over the red raw remains of what looked like half a cow. Survive, I suppose that's the best you can expect here.

'You brought a bottle,' said Tracey, tottering to the door, opening it six inches and peering out at us.

'Just our ghoolies,' I said. I think perhaps this is a Geordie expression, circa 1960, which I picked up from my dad.

'You what?' said Tracey.

'You what, you what, you what, you what, you what!' shouted Lol, clapping his hands in time to that inane North Bank rhythm. I'm a fan of football chants, and I hope at King's College Cambridge, when I get there as a Senior Wally, for my postgraduate PhD thrombosis I'll do a dissertation on the symbolism of football songs, but this 'You What' lark really is stupid. Perhaps that's the point.

'Oh it's you, Cartner, come in,' said Tracey, undoing a three-foot-thick door chain. 'I see you've brought your minder.'

'He goes back to Broadmoor tomorrow,' I said. 'It's his last night out.'

'Where's the drink then?' said Lol, pushing his way forward, shoving his hand up Tracey's skirt as he passed her, which wasn't difficult to do as she was wearing what appeared to be a tight leather belt, about six inches long, hardly enough to cover her.

'Get lost,' said Tracey.

'I could in there,' said Lol. 'Room enough for half the sixth form, as we all know.'

'He's so crude, that Lawrence,' said Tracey. 'I don't know why you hang around with him.'

'The consultant asked me to. When you've had electric shock treatment, it does take a while to get over it.'

'Here, have some of this, me and Karen made it.'

She dipped a large ladle into a bowl of rotting fruit and vegetables and brought up a large ladle, full of rotting fruit and vegetables, which she announced was a punch, courtesy of *Woman's Journal*.

'Do I drink it or open a greengrocer's?'

'Cheeky beggar,' she said, but smiled, gave me a little peck on the cheek, leaving three layers of 'Lily of the valley' on my best button-down shirt collar, then went back to dancing with Karen. The two of them were all in black, which was quite cunning really. At least you could see them, make out who they were against the multi-coloured violence of the room's fitted carpet and the clashing patterns of the wallpaper.

I sat down on a sofa, but the wrong one apparently, or the wrong way, because Tracey came across and took away a pink cushion from behind my back.

'Me dad'll kill me if that gets mucked up.'

I don't go to a lot of orgies, well I do have a heck of a lot of homework, but from what I've read in the *Sunday Sport* it's sort of well, free play, anything goes. Worrying about pink cushions was not a reassuring sign. Perhaps there would be more fun at Arlington House tonight.

I carefully arranged my feet on the centre of the loudest patterns, hoping the drips would be concealed. It was an immaculate flat, everything spotless, everything new, everything paid for. Well, her dad is a taxi driver with his own cab. He'd gone off skiing with his fancy woman, as he does every New Year, though not always the same fancy woman, or even the same ski resort.

There were only eight people at the party so far, three of Tracey's friends, including two girls dressed like Christmas turkeys waiting to be stuffed, sorry, Lol-type remark, but oh so true, plus me and Lol and two kids in shades. One of them's called Adrian, used to be a right little Mummy's boy, now look at him, lives in our street, so I know for a fact he's only fifth year, flaming cheek. He and his mate are both budding dealers, so it's said, and the way Tracey was screaming and yelling at them, it was obvious she'd heard the same stories.

'If there's one thing my dad won't allow, it's druggies,' Tracey kept on yelling. That makes two things, pet. Any marks on the pinko cushions, plus druggies. I don't know which is worse.

Lol was telling the two non-dancing turkeys that he really loved Boy George and no, you haven't really got 'The Best of Wham!' have you, this is too much, hey, that's not a Michael Jackson is it, fantastic, let's have it on at once, that's if you won't get too excited, ladies, no, really, no kidding, he's my all-time favourite, wow.

He went across to change the ghetto-blaster, one of the smaller ones that only needs four people and a lorry to take it to parties, giving a huge sigh as he passed me, as if overcome with emotion and pleasure at the company and good taste and fab punch and groovy choice of records.

I never saw him again that night. He put on a Michael Jackson at full volume, then just disappeared. With one hand he opened the flat door, chain and all, and with the other he turned up the volume, then he was gone. I was the only one who saw him go. Well, there wasn't much else to feast my eyes on. You can see two dopey girls dancing together in our Common Room any old time.

'I wouldn't stuff them with yours,' was Lol's final farting

shot. I distinctly heard it. And a great belch. They're his two party tricks. For an encore, he sets fire to his fart. Perhaps just as well he'd gone early. No doubt it will amuse them at Arlington House. They don't get many top variety turns these days.

When Tracey realized he had gone, she screamed and yelled abuse, the rotten sod, last time she was inviting him, not that she had, the slob had invited himself.

The two junior dealers sat in silence, trying to look cool, acting hard, looking stoned. I've noticed that the next generation of yobs coming up hardly speak. Our generation, the ones who fought in the Great War of O-levels, who saw service before GCSEs were ever thought of, were much noisier and more outgoing. Could it be the weed? They took it in with their mother's milk and it's knocked all the energy out of them. Or perhaps behind those Woolworth's shades they were sound asleep. Not bad judges, considering the party.

That left me on my own, the only masculine, as opposed to mescaline, factor. In a dull light, Tracey has a certain *je ne sai quan*, that's a French obscenity that Silas told us, but I might have got it slightly wrong. When he does pass on jokes, they're all so erudite or tri-lingual that I can never understand them, far less remember them.

If I had to, really had to, 'cos they were the only four women left on the planet, which order would I have them in, with or without a side salad?

'Some more punch, Cartner.'

'You trying to get me drunk?' I said.

'No, the waste-disposal's bust, so I've gotta get rid of this stuff before me dad gets back tomorrow.'

Was that a joke? Could be. Her gang has this fierce approach to everything, loud-mouthed and violent, and you can't tell if they're about to murder each other, or wet themselves laughing because it's all been some take-off from

34

EastEnders that I've missed. I did notice a waste-disposal unit. More than we've got, but then we are the deprived lower middle classes, doomed to cycle through life and eat muesli. I'd also noticed a luxury bathroom, on my tour of the happy home between drinks, with a sunken, circular plunge bath in avocado green, complete with suggestive-looking nozzles, and a new Wilton carpet, bougainvillaea purple, so deep and thick you could grow cannabis in it.

I was not allowed to go into her dad's bedroom, on any condition. I asked if one of his fancy women was lying there, waiting for sir to come home and pleasure her in his snow-boots, just like the Duke of Wellington. This got complicated 'cos she presumed the Duke of Wellington was the pub. Is that what happens when they close? Dirty sods.

Her dad recently bought the flat from the council, following the guidance of his heroine in life, M. Thatcher. Seemed daft to me. Why stay here, in this dump? Perhaps he's grown fond of the lift or feared he would miss the friendly neighbourhood Alsatians.

I began to feel a bit sick, what with the noise and the clash of colours and the turkeys cackling like old women.

'I'll just have a walk round the block,' I said. 'Clear the old head.'

'You're not going are you?' said Tracey. 'You're the only bloke left, apart from those two jerks.'

'Thanks. Not a lot of competition. No, I won't be long. Then it will be time for Norwich.'

'Norwich, Cartner? You're not walking that far are you?'

'Nickers Off Ready When I Come Home,' I said. 'Haven't you heard that? What sort of school did you go to? I think we learned that in Miss Button's. Oh, but you were always off sick.'

She went back to tell Karen and the turkeys this ancient gem, and I could hear the raucous cackling. What has happened to girls these days? Sez is just the same. They all laugh at double volume. Bring back gentle, ladylike giggling. So unseemly this loud displaying of their feathers, aggressive laughter, drawing attention to themselves, daring the world to tell them off. And the language of modern women, my dears, the language.

Do I feel threatened? Are we blokes being usurped, demoted, de-knackered? We now have some skinhead girls in the fourth year who've perfected belching. Is nothing safe, is nothing sacred. No wonder we're all becoming more feminine. I'm now about the only bloke in the whole sixth form who can't cook a meal for himself.

Back to the scene of the *crime passionel*. (That's the worst of telling it to you later, old Wee Pee. I keep going off at tangents. There should be an inbuilt screen on which everything is instantly recorded as it happens, so you just press E for EDIT and it flashes up on the screen, without your having to tap it out. Oh, forgot. God gave us one. Memory.)

I staggered around, looking for the exit, trying to find the street door to step out of. I had forgotten I was on the seventeenth floor. That sobered me up, coming face to face with seventeen floors of fresh air, concrete and instant death.

I sat down for a bit to get my balance and find my ball bearings, then slowly and sensibly I tried to remember where the hell the lift was. All I wanted was to get home. Imagine, a chap of my refined tastes and sensibilities, wasting a precious Saturday night with a load of Wendies. I might even have fallen asleep for a bit, because when I looked around again, more soberly, I could distinctly hear noise from the lift shaft, only about twenty yards away, that horrible machine slowly grinding its sordid way upwards. I managed to stand up and make my way towards it.

Out of the lift stepped Isabella and a tall black bloke. She was carrying what looked like a case. They turned away from me, walking quickly in the other direction.

Bloody hell. What am I saving myself for? What is that mirage I am pursuing? What I am doing with my life, my art, my willy? Nothing, is the simple answer.

'Hi Tracey, it's me, let me in, I feel better now, thanks for asking.'

She was instantly all over me, her wet lips down my neck, her arms curled round me, her legs rubbing my calves, her feet playing footsie.

'Hell, Cart. Where was you? Your feet are soakin'. What you been doing? Not wet yourself, have ya?'

'It's raining outside,' I said.

'Well gerremoff,' she yelled. The whole room was now packed, so I must have fallen asleep outside. There were even more turkeys present than before, one or two of them very drunk. Some of them heard Tracey's last remark and started clapping and yelling, expecting some real party fun at last. Someone even turned down the music.

'Gerremoff,' repeated Tracey, at the top of her voice. All the turkeys took up the same cry. Was there going to be a gang-bang, with little me being the one about to be banged by all these screaming viragos? That's one of my two recurring nightmares. I sat down and very solemnly took off my trainers, then I stood up, bowed, said 'thank you ladies and gentlemen, you've been a lovely audience.' Then I fell over, completely zonked out.

I woke up on this bed, about the size of the Albert Hall, all gilt and chintz, the sort Louis XIV must have used for guest nights. I felt really rotten.

Very slowly I looked around. I caught a glimpse of this pathetic, tired, worn-out creature staring at me, so I closed my eyes. This time, on regaining consciousness, I looked up at the ceiling. The same pathetic figure was staring back at me. I know that physog, I said, seen it somewhere before, remind me. I know that physog, repeated the lips on my face in the mirror.

Not just one mirror. Even the floors had mirrors. Tracey's dad must be a hell of a feller.

'Oh, you're awake now, Cartner,' said Tracey, coming into the bedroom, closing the door and locking it from the inside. 'How you feeling, lovey?'

'Ohhh,' I groaned.

She sat down on the bed beside me and began taking off her tights, wriggling out of them like best pork from a sausage skin. One bit stuck, as it always does, hanging on to her big toe. She had to give it an extra hard pull, falling back on the bed beside me. I gave another groan. Agony, not ecstasy.

'Oh, poor you, little Cartner. Shall I get you some Alka-Seltzer?'

'No, s'all right. Just give me a moment to – to get myself together.'

Was I still asleep? Was it a dream? I'd imagined this enough times in the last decade, on the job like a raging bull, hold me back, I'm a wild stallion, but now in reality all I could think about was where's me clothes, who took them off, and if anyone's nicked me last trainers, what am I going to tell me mum?

She was naked, completely, except for her six-inch black leather skirt. Argh. Ahh. Arrghh. Ahhhhh. I pulled the sheet up over my head. If she takes that off, it'll be too late. I'm only young. I'm only little. Help.

She was now sitting at a large kidney-shaped walnut table, slowly brushing her hair in front of a line of spotlights, three tiers of them, as if she were in the number one dressing room at the London Palladium, getting ready for another virtuoso performance. She seemed so calm and confident. So did her body.

I'd always presumed from her frothy, phoney exterior that she would be all thin and delicate, even scrawny, suspecting that the cleavage was all part of the package, bought off the peg at Top Girl, which she took off at bedtime with the rest of the tinsel and wrapping. Though what do I know about girls' real bodies? The *Dandy* never drew any, and in 2000 AD it's all a joke.

'How you doing?' she said, turning at the table to look at me, casual but kindly, composed but concerned. A workaday girl, I thought. A matter-of-fact, just-another-day girl. A going-to-work-on-an-egg girl, or, in this case, on a wimp.

She dropped her brush and had to lean over from her stool to pick it up. I could hardly bear it.

She is kind, I thought, a treasure at heart. She's not being raucous or vulgar. On her own, she's obviously a decent, loving, friendly sort. And she must like me. It is her dad's precious bedroom. She wouldn't infringe that with just anyone. Pity she's not a bit brighter, but who needs that? Where does that get you, what difference does that make, when you get down to – well, it?

I heard a soft plop and I opened half an eye to see that finally she'd let her skirt drop. Smiling weakly but defiantly she walked over to the bed, pulled back the sheet where I was cowering and smiling weakly myself, and got in beside me.

There was a sudden loud and violent cough. She sat up and spat out some chewing-gum. Oh, the romance of it all. She pulled down the sheet once again, got out of bed, walked across the room and picked up the offending chewing-gum where it had lodged itself in the deep-pile Wilton. Lest Pater be upset. Then the process began again, her coming back to bed and getting in beside me. I had a crick in my neck just from watching her.

'What about, you know,' I muttered. There was a long silence.

'Me dad? Don't worry. He's not back till tomorrow morning.'

'No, I mean, you know, taking care.'

'Condoms, you mean. Give over. I've been on the Pill since I was twelve.'

'No, I mean what about, I was wondering about, Aids . . .'

'Ade's? Ade's got Karen. She's waiting for him in my bedroom. I think he's horrible, personally, a real turn-off. I've always fancied you, you know, right from Miss Button's. I wanted to show you everything that day, but I got caught, my first, now was I nine or ten when it first happened? I know it was a Monday, cos . . .'

Dear God. I realize women are meant to make the running these days, take the dominant role, but bloody hell, you'd think they'd improve their pillow-talk. I hate that sort of women's chat anyway, always have done. I don't want all that stuff mentioned. I also hate seeing any of Sez's scruffy underclothes or personal effects, which she will leave lying around the house till I could scream. Am I a prude? Am I a prune? Give me a bit of subtlety, please, not this full-frontal approach. Let's have some mysteries. Not this coarse conversation.

'Do you want any help, lovey?' she said, putting her hand down under the sheet. God, are there no secrets left, no privacies in this permissive world?

'No, thank you,' I said, giving a contented sigh, or similar. 'Everything's triffic. Just one thing, though.'

'Yes, Cartner. What is it, Cartner?'

I hate people who use your Christian name all the time, so creepy, so phoney, so American. Don't I seem so full of hate these days.

'Anything you want, Cartner,' she said simpering, in what she thought was a sexy voice, giving me a little squeeze under the sheet.

'I hardly dare mention it,' I said. 'As it's all so groovy. But could you possibly see your way to putting off half a dozen or so of those spotlights? It's like the operating theatre at the Royal Free in here. You're not shooting it on the video, are you?'

'Funny you should say that, Cartner. Me dad once did that, but it was all out of focus. Made a real mess of it, he did.'

'You mean he filmed himself here, on the . . .'

'Oooh, not him on the job. Can't bear to think of that, it's creepy, don't you think, at their age?'

'I don't believe it happens,' I said. 'Once you get to forty, everything falls off, from your hair to your how'syourfath-er . . .'

'Is that true?'

'Yup, I read it in my mum's *Pears Cyclopaedia*. Anyway, what was your dad filming on the video, eh?'

'It was just me, bringing him his breakfast in bed. I was about ten at the time and I had to dress up as a French maid. Ever so sweet. We often show it, if we're on our own.'

I looked at her for any signs of a snigger, or shame, but she was smiling radiantly, even fragrantly. She was very clean, I will say that, body-wise, but her psyche could be a bit murkier. What had happened in her little life? I could be venturing down paths more interesting than I had expected, but I think I'd prefer not to go there. Spare me any family confessions, things she might regret telling me, truths that might bind me to her. I'm only here for the beer. Wish I'd had some, not that rotten punch.

'Come on then, Trace,' I said. 'Close your eyes and think of England.'

'Not the cricket team, I hope,' she said. 'Or the football. Load of tossers, all of them, though I quite fancy that Peter Shilton, I bet he's got a really hairy chest . . .'

Oh no. I'll have to put a stop to all this. I can hardly wait any longer. Here we go then, Cartner old son, your starter for one, which is about the only amount you'll manage. Starting off not with a bang or a bonk but a little whimper. I wonder if she'll even notice.

'What you giggling at?' said Tracey.

'Nothing, nothing, just keep those eyes closed, you're going to get a very big surprise. Well, perhaps a medium-sized prize, even a small to medium . . .'

There was a gigantic crash and a whole wall seemed to fall towards us. I thought at first that the flat was collapsing, another Sixties tower-block hits the dust, or that it was an earthquake, or an IRA bomb. But it was only some double louvered doors on a wall-to-wall fitted wardrobe, just beside the bed, which had suddenly been thrown open. Out of them stepped Karen, stark naked.

'You stupid bitch!' yelled Tracey. 'I told you MY bedroom.'

I was up and out of bed. I found my clothes on the floor, pulled my trousers on in a panic and ran from the bedroom and straight out of the flat. I tore all the way down those seventeen flights of stairs, not wishing to wait, or face that lift.

It was only when I got to the ground level and emerged out into the street that I realized I'd left my trainers behind.

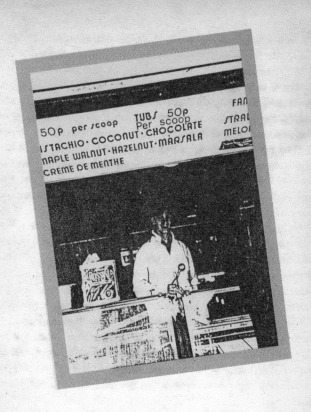

4 A Hard Day's Work, but an Unusual Ending

I was cycling to work on the first day of Spring-like Spring and naturally a young man's fancy gently turns to thoughts of fancying older women, any older women, not simply one in particular.

I'd decided that's where I should begin, start with a bit of experience and sophistication, not waste myself on some screeching, yelling, callow, silly, pushy, aggressive, vulgar wannabe who just thinks of her hair and love-comics and *Top of the Pops*.

There was one stunner at the traffic lights, looking really great, not standing by them but sitting in her Porsche, talking on the phone, watching herself in the mirror talking on the phone. I gazed down into her lap, observed the gentle fold of her perfectly kept black skirt and her long silky legs about to caress the accelerator, legs that could caress me, start off my accelerator, and I thought hey up, Cart, this image will keep you going for quite a few weeks, when the mind wanders from the old WP.

I always avert my gaze in the newsagent's from that top row of blatant porn, or try to; sometimes you can't, it sort of jumps out at you, even when you're not looking, buying a notebook, an ice lolly, or even passing on the other side of the street. Honestly, that sort of hairy stuff just revolts me. I have, of course, seen far worse, only in photies, the sort of stuff Lol passes around. It always scares me, rather than excites me. But a subtle hint of a subtle shape from a fully clothed lady, then wow, I'm away, which of course can be rather awkward when you're riding a bike. You become convinced the whole world can see and is sniggering and pointing.

She turned and gazed upwards, straight through me, as if I did not exist. I realized she was simply checking out her other profile in her wing mirror. And why not? Probably about to chair a vital meeting, sack a few thousand men, invest a couple of billion.

Square, padded shoulders though, hmm, not so keen on them, a fashion I've never liked, why do they do it? But the thought calmed me down, got me back to normal and off the boil. And so off I cycled, clip clop, clip clop, tell me, what onomatopoetic noise does a bike make? And how do you spell it? This stupid WP is no help. It does have a spelling thing, LOCOSPELL, so it boasts, but gawd know how it works.

I tried to decide whether I should spend the afternoon riding round the City, hoping to be picked up, instead of round Camden Town, ruining my right hand once again. It's been hell all week at school, especially trying to write with a cheapo Biro. My best Parker pen, bought by my gran at Christmas, has disappeared. Not my fault. They'll nick anything at our school. Fall asleep in the Common Room and they'll have the pants off you. And that's not just the girls.

I could hardly put my brakes on for the pain in my right wrist. Why ever did I agree to have a Saturday job as a brain surgeon? My little hands are just not up to all that effort.

Around the age of thirty, I think that should do, don't want them too ancient. How old was Mrs Robinson? That was the late-night movie the other night, really good, I fancied her as well. But none of my friends' Mums look anything like her, and I've considered them all.

That reminds me, a remind I was trying to forget. My mum's just done something really revolting, for which I'll never forgive her. How can she, at her age, in her condition, with what she thinks passes for a figure? She's bought herself a leotard. Sez agrees with me for once. We're both leaving home, should she ever put it on while we're on the same planet.

I wonder if I'll ever make it as a toy-boy. But who'd want to toy with me? In fact, people don't see me, that's why they carve me up on my bike, on the pavement, on the rocky road through life. Sometimes I think I've just imagined me. If I left the stage, there would be no gap. Where have I been, what have I done, why did I bother? I have used up very little oxygen, Mr God. I was never a bother to you.

Ah well, only ten minutes late. Dimitri will try to stop my pay. Marie will moan and groan as ever. The queues will be enormous. My right hand aches and a drowsy numbness pains my arse and this thumb still has not healed from last week's operations. Sorry, Sister, you'll have to close the operating theatre this afternoon. Doctor Livingstone will do all the heart transplants tomorrow instead.

Should I advertise in the *Exchange and Mart*, toy-boy available, photographs can be sent, anything considered, must have long silky legs. But Mum would open all the letters, she always does, even special offers ('You have won £10,000 in a car competition, here is your lucky number'), then she licks them and seals them back up, every one. It's to give Little Cartner the exciting pleasure of opening his very own post. Pathetic. I don't get any real post. How can I, when I don't exist?

They can take their pick today. Any woman can choose any toy-boy she likes. All these desirable thirty-year-olds, and the forty-year-olds for that matter, and very soon it'll be every geriatric who can climb out of her wheelchair, they'll all be having their little bit on the side. I read some really frightening figures in the *Independent* this morning. (I don't usually admit I read it, which I don't, except for the football, and I keep up this non-stop attack on the OF for having given up the *Guardian*.) According to the Family Policy Studies Circle, or some such nonsense, there will be 284,000 more marriageable males than females in the year 1993. They're talking about me, my generation. Why did I get the male card? I'm on a loser. There will just be too many of us around, cluttering up the earth, cluttering up the dole queues, crowding the Lonely Hearts columns. Even the ugliest, thickest woman will be able to take her pick. And they'll go for Lol, I just know it.

Why didn't I take my chance with Tracey? It will be too late soon, once they all find out these boring facts. They won't need to bother with the likes of me. Good job she doesn't read the *Independent*. But the *Sun* will pick it up soon. Then I won't be asked again. I'm on the shelf. And my sell-by date has already expired.

'Sorry Dim, I gotta puncture, and there was this accident, this posh woman, I had to rescue her from her Porsche, and then . . .'

I saw him write down the precise time, the rotten pig. I parked my bike at the back and went into the staff room. I knew Marie would be watching me and going, tut tut tut, like the old biddy she is, shaking her head but enjoying it, as if she were Madame Défarge at the tumbrel. That's the novel we're doing. How could I forget it? Only three months to go, and the whole world will find out how little I know about it, or about anything. Especially without my good pen.

It's a laff, the staff room, about one metre square and not enough room to swing a kebab, but the Brute Brothers, Dimitri and Georgi, insist that's what we must call it.

I breathed in, to give myself space, then put on my white operating coat. Scalpels, Matron, forceps please, no, this won't hurt. We have only the finest surgeons here.

They've got it into their heads to go upmarket, God knows why, so the part-time boys like me have to wear white over-alls and the staff waiters are in red jackets. It's still the same greasy Greek caff it's always been, but it means they can put up all the prices.

It's all a rip-off, just like life. The sweated labour, the disgusting conditions, the insecurity, the pointlessness. But what a lucky boy I am to work here, to have a job in this day and age. The O F and the O W keep on telling me this. And it's true.

I had to wait years to get it, grease my way up the waiting list, yes, sir, no, sir to Dim. Georgi's the nice one, always fair with the money, but he's more interested in clothes and cars and imagining he's in Wham! Now there's another dust-covered blast from the past. Dim does most of the work, and he's a real bully. I don't have regular hours, just have to be available every Saturday and Sunday. They let me know during the week what shift I'm on. If I refuse too many times, that will be it, and Sez will never forgive me.

The only reason she is occasionally civilized to me is because she hopes, when I go, to inherit the earth, or at least my job. After I've gone off to 'Varsity, or the tech, or the DHSS, or some squat, or off my rocker, or whatever it is I'll be going off to in the autumn, she thinks she'll take over. Fat chance. They wouldn't have her, the lazy slob. She's never had a job in her life. They're so spoiled this modern generation, especially the so-called female of the specious.

The feeble sun, rather weedy, rather phoney with little warmth in it, had brought out the crowds. It meant I was straight on to the ice-cream. And me with my poorly thumb as well. Better than the cappuccino machine. I still hate that. I wasn't allowed on it for weeks, as it has a will of its own and has attacked several people over the years, splurting volcanic water everywhere, then finishing them off with the infra-red steam torture. Not that Dim cares. All he moans about is the expense of the repairs when it explodes, while you're standing there with both arms burned off.

I've now passed out, cappuccino trained, flying colours, mentioned in dispatches by Marie, but I'll never be allowed inside the restaurant proper, to rise to a red jacket and take orders from our esteemed customers. That's for the all-time greats, the professionals, the full-time slaves. I am condemned to the front counter doing ices and coffees, but I know my place in the order of things. And sometimes Marie, so-called manageress of the front counter, is kind and slips me a block of maple walnut, or pistachio, just as I'm getting on my bike to go home. She always seems to choose those

48

days when I've already nicked several blocks of crème de menthe and pistachio, and my jumper is jam-packed and my trousers pockets are full.

I used to think she was Dim and Georgi's mum, as she looked about sixty when I first saw her, but she's not quite as old as that. She's just some distant relation they've taken pity on, one of the many people who cower in the bowels of the café. I once had to go down to the cellars to stack some drums of oil, and I saw three off-duty waiters asleep on a shelf, laid out as neatly as coffins, their pathetic belongings beside them. At least they were in England, land of opportunity and freedom, where there's enormous potential for any immigrants to work themselves to death for the mingiest pittance.

And so to work. It's the rotten scoop that does it. If I worked there every day, I might get calluses on the calluses, but I always have a week to recover, during which time my poor little thumb and forefinger think they've been let off and try to grow soft and tender again, as nature intended them to be, then wham bam comes Saturday, and they get pummelled and crippled once again.

Is there a metaphor there, hmm? Is perhaps life like that? Should I try a PASTE or even a CUT and see what comes up on the screen? No, you're in luck. I'll let you off. At that moment in came Isabella.

Oh, my little heart, oh, my little corpuscles, slow down please, I'm too young to pass out.

Isabella was at the end of the queue. She had not seen me, but then why should she, still a stranger round here, new to the area, new to my life, and in this white coat (complete with raspberry bloodstains) I could be anyone from the Muppet Chef to Jack the Ripper.

I thought about hiding till she'd gone, or asking Marie to serve for a bit, say I'm feeling faint. Marie is quite good that way, always interested in anyone's disease or illness.

49

Hold on, steady, cool it, Cart, think on, this could be your little chance. I might be able to ingratiate myself and charm her, or just impress my delightful presence upon her. A lot of people in the sixth form have become my bestest friends since I've begun working here. Oh, the power, the glory, not to mention the corruption, that's all possible when you're in charge of the ice-cream.

'What eeze eet, Catner,' said Marie. She's never got my name straight. 'Okay you?'

How perceptive of her. Must be the sweat running down my forehead meeting the sweat pouring out of my battered thumb, mixing with the beat of my thudding heart.

I nodded that I was fine, fine, muttering, no problem, no problem, Marie's favourite expression, every foreigner's favourite expression and one I've vowed never to use again. I found myself giving the wrong change to a line of little kids, mixing up the orders, trying desperately hard to work out what I was going to say to Her.

A deep, chunky, masculine silence might be suitable, with a few moody looks thrown in. But what if she doesn't even recognize me? Some smart remarks, perhaps, bit of the old patter, that might be the thing. What can I give you, darling, fancy a little scoop? I'll put something nice in your cone for you, or would you like one of my specials, huh? No, that's too crude.

'Hello, Cartner. I didn't know you worked here.'

She knows my name. O rapture, bliss to be alive and in this white, spattered coat, it's very heaven to serve you, my blessed.

'Don't actually work,' I said, shaking my right hand and sighing. 'I'm doing thumb exercises. I'm hoping it'll grow really huge so I can take it on tour and charge people to look at it.'

'Yes, it must be rather painful.'

Wait a mo, Cart. You don't want to appear a moaner and complainer, a weakling with puny fingers do you?

'So what will it be?' I said snappily, on the ball, ever so brisk and efficient we working chaps. 'You look like a coffee person to me.'

'That's right, but just a small one.'

'No problem,' I said, thinking, yup, small ones are me all right. But I said nothing, getting on with the main performance, trying to put as much panache as possible into doling out fifty pence worth of ice-cream. Not a lot of scope, in a scoop. What if it all drops out, or the cone breaks, or I let it slip? Oh, you wouldn't believe the things that can go wrong with such a simple operation.

I must have been frowning with the intensity of it all. I realized she was smiling, amused at my seriousness. So I smiled back, amused at her amusement. Oh, what communication can be passed in a smile, what feeling conveyed in a look. Or was I imagining it?

She passed over her money, and I passed it back, then she passed it over the counter again. Is she thick, or what? Dim scuttled behind the counter in his bossy way, so I had to pick up the money and appear to go to the till, wait till he'd gone, then slide her money back across the counter. She must think I'm the one who's thick.

'Thanks,' she said, licking her ice-cream. 'See you.'

'Hope so,' I said, watching her leave. I wanted to lick her steps, suck her sensible flat shoes, taste the flavour of her coffee-coloured man's donkey jacket, savour the line of her cone-shaped jeans, enjoy every hair on her prize-winning head, all natural ingredients, no artificial colouring.

'Whose moneys this is?' said Marie, all quizzical. She hates any irregularities in the till, always fearful that Dim is going to accuse her of fiddling the cash.

So she hadn't picked it up. Was it deliberate, not wanting

to be beholden to me or to receive any favours? Or is she one of these high moral people who don't approve of the fiddlingest fiddle. I used to be like that, till I started work. Now I know it's how the world runs. All jobs have their fiddle rate. The trick is to use it but not abuse it – well, not too much.

I worked the rest of the afternoon in a dream, a daze. I'd blown it, thrown away my chance. She must have nothing else do to, coming here for an ice-cream, all on her own, unless she was on the way somewhere. I should have jumped over the counter and said, let's go girl. Let me take you away from all this squalor, we can make our own squalor together.

Dim would have been furious if I'd suddenly left my post, but hard Cheddar. Who cares about that lousy job? Or any rotten job. That's the main reason why I'm now so keen to get to college, any sort of college. Imagine having to go straight out to work from school. Anything to avoid that, to put off the hierarchies, the fawning, the creeping, the grind and pointlessness of it all, the day-after-day boring drudgeries, just to earn a living. I know there won't be a job out there that I'll actually enjoy, that's too much, and ditto the Lovely Ms Rightish, whom I used to think must be out there. There's probably nothing at all waiting for me.

'Before you do go, Carner,' said Marie, 'could you plis take zeez down to zee cold store, then I have zomezink for you.' (Oh, let's forget that corny Radio Four foreign talk. I'm fed up with having to keep looking for the zeds.)

I was just getting my bike out and unlocking the chain, ready to zoom home. Now I had to hump several large boxes into the cold room, which I hate, just to please Marie. I always think I'm going to be locked in, that the door will slam and no one will know where I am, then I'll just freeze, extremities first, dropping off one by one like icicles, then the inner organs, then the blood will turn solid, the heart will freeze over, the bloody Dimitri will have won again. Another part-timer who left without collecting all his wages. At least he'd paid this time, thanks to Marie's reminding him.

She was nowhere to be seen when I came back to the counter. Two of the older waiters were sweeping the floors. One of them pointed towards the back, saying Marie was waiting for me.

I never thought she might live on the premises, but then I never thought about her living anywhere, just accepted her as part of the furniture, washed and cleaned and put away every night in a drawer along with the scoops. Need a big drawer, with her weight.

I came to a little yard I didn't know was there and heard her call my name through a small door. I went in and it was a remarkably cosy bed-sitter, arranged like a little shrine with pictures of Jesus everywhere, glossy prints of the Virgin, biblical scenes, very clean plastic flowers and tall, ornate, ornamental vases, the sort you win at a fairground if you're unlucky and don't get the coconuts.

Marie appeared, dressed in what looked like a kimono, or it could have been her dressing-gown. Oh my God. It's the Older Woman. Let me out.

'Come here, my leetle boy,' she said, grabbing me by the hand and closing her door with the other. 'I have something specially for you, I keep it for you, you not seen anything like thees before.'

Well, that covers quite a lot. After all, what have *I* seen? You could surprise me with almost anything, but please, Mother of God, not that, anything but, Holy Mary, I promise to be good for ever, if only you spare me.

She was bending down, looking in a chest of drawers. I could smell moth-balls and see faded newspapers and neatly folded underclothes in every drawer, some of them rather saucy, as seen in the discreet ads of the so-called posh papers.

What was she doing, buying such stuff at her age? She must be, well, hmm, let's reassess this, now that I'm being forced to stand beside her, close up, and am being offered hints of her ample bosom and can see bits of her ample flesh, stuff I didn't think she ever carried. Well, you don't when you work beside someone you take to be a drudge, someone who's always been stuck in a horrible red overall. She could be just forty. Old as the crow's-feet fly, but not too over the top, not too old to tango. What am I saying, what am I thinking? I must get out of here. But if I struggle or push her away or unclasp her hand, which is still gripping mine, she might scream or turn nasty and I'd be accused of assault. Poor old soul, she had been kind to me.

'Ah, here it eez,' she announced in triumph, taking out an old, faded folder containing what looked like photographs. Please, God, it's nothing dodgy, nothing lewd or blue, I couldn't bear it, I was in the Boy Scouts for well over a week. I made my vows to be pure in thought, word and deed, so I must not be led into any sort of temptation.

'Look at this, this is exciting, ees it not?'

I put my hand over my eyes in a pretend mock horror, but meaning it, expecting to be horrored, then mocked.

I opened my eyes slowly to find the faces of the A C Milan team of 1972 staring at me. Eighteen swarthy blokes, plus one who looked like an Icelander, all in cheap, nasty colour, overlapping and badly matching, now going yellow at the edges.

Marie solemnly unwrapped another package and presented me with an A C Milan banner, a badge, a pennant, a glossy handbook and a bundle of programmes.

'I know you just love your football, Cantner.'

'Hey, this is triffic, Marie,' I said, very relieved. 'I'll treasure these for ever, very kind of you.'

I got them under my arm, released her grip and started to move backwards, hoping to make my way out of the room.

'Have a leetle drink,' she said, pulling a bottle from behind a chair and pouring two glasses of what looked like thick sugar. 'Dont-a rush, everyone in English is rushing.'

After such a present, I couldn't just rush off, could I? I am human and not totally insensitive and ungrateful. Which, of course, was a mistake.

She began to pour out her whole life story and most of the bottle. Her kimono started to droop lower on her shoulders, her thighs becoming more in evidence as she continually crossed and recrossed her fat legs. Then she stood up and began leaning all over me, which was when I realized she was naked underneath. And I also realized what she was expecting. I'm not slow all the time.

I've put D E L for delete through the next bit. Sorry about that. Can't take any chances. Some day the O F might crack the secrets of his own W P. No, that's not the reason. I did put it all up there on the flickering box, warts and all, oh God, the warts, and it made me feel exorcized. But I now want it all wiped from my mind. And wiped from the screen.

I'm still what I call intacto, honest, pure as the driven slush, but what a near escape. Why ever did I fancy the older woman? As if I haven't got enough fancies and fantasies to be going on with. Stick to your own age, Cart, your own cage, your own rage.

Then watch this page. But how can you? Ha, ha, ha, it's all in the machine, all in the mind.

5 Protest, Politics and Posters, Finishing with Crumpets

I'm sleeping in on Saturday mornings. Well, what else is there to do. I'd like to sleep in for the whole week, the whole term, perhaps a whole life, just in case the next one coming along is any better.

I've lost my job. Dim has told me to get my cards, whatever they are. I think he forgot I wasn't properly employed. He just said, that's it, I don't want you to work here again.

He maintains I rang and said I wanted more money or else, that it was exploitation and slave labour, all of which I believe, probably even said it to people at work, but I would never dare say it to his rotten face. This was all in some message, purporting to be from me. It was obviously Marie, her way of getting her own back, which I can understand. It means I'm jobless, penniless, unable to buy new trainers or even a pen.

My Saturdays are now free. But there's not much you can do on Saturdays that's also free. Hmm, there is something I can do today, which I half said I would. Suppose I might as well half get up.

'You can make your own breakfast, can't you, Cartner?' said the OW, full of sarcasm, all wasted on me, as centuries of practice have helped me to rise above their sneers and jeers at my domestic uselessness.

'Why can't you?' I said, dragging myself into the kitchen, half expecting a belt round the ear'oles.

'Because I'm going out, that's why,' she said.

'But it's in the contract. You agreed to be my Mum. I never asked you. You've got to see it through. You started this thing. Any toast? Oh God. I didn't ask to be born. You've got to finish it, and that means looking after me, doing everything . . . Ouch! That hurt.'

This solid lump had hit me on the side of the head. Not at all funny. Could have been dangerous. Could have damaged what little brain I have and ruined all my A-level chances. I picked it up from the floor. A solid croissant, still in its plastic, still frozen.

'You know what to do with it. Regulo One. In the oven for ten minutes. I don't have to do a drawing, do I?'

It's been a tradition in our family that on Saturdays we have our only breakfast of the week, hot croissants and real coffee, yum yum. During the week it's free play, each human for him or herself, which means we get nothing unless we make it ourselves. As the O W goes out to work, she sees no reason why she should make breakfast for us. I maintain she should make half a breakfast for us, as she only does a half-job, as a Point Five primary-school teacher.

On Saturdays she usually does knock her little self out, putting the croissants in the oven, big deal, and we usually all have a leisurely breakfast together. That was the olden days. This is now. So she says.

'Where you going, anyway?' I asked.

'Do I have to tell you again? Sometimes you can be so annoying.'

'Oh come on, all the time, surely. I do try hard at it.'

'You know it's the first morning of my new class,' she said. 'And I don't want to be late.'

'Oh no, these late developers, mature students, middle-aged old biddies,' I groaned. 'Pathetic, all of them. You've got work here. No need to drag yourself off to some boring class to learn about boring old . . .'

I had been told, but now I'd forgotten. French, was it? No, that was last term. Fancy salads? She did mutter something about that. Or was it car mechanics? Nope, she can't drive. Could it be photography? She can't take photies either, but she has nicked the O F's camera.

'Oh well,' I said opening the oven, 'keeps you off the streets I suppose . . .'

'Not with the plastic still on, you fool,' she suddenly shouted, just as I was shoving it in. 'And let it heat up first.'

'Just testing,' I said, lying.

'You are just so lazy and selfish. Why can't you put two in? Do one for Sez as well. She'll be down in a minute.'

'Why should I? What does she do for me? I didn't ask her to be my sister. Nobody asked me if I wanted her to be born. Nobody . . . ouch! That hurt.'

This time she hit me with what appeared to be a camera

case, just as I was bending down, putting both croissants in the oven.

'And I don't want to see any mess when I come home,' she said, going down the hall and out of the front door.

'Well don't look then,' I said.

Sez came down in what looked like her dressing-gown, which I always hate, seeing either her or the OW half dressed. Disgusting, if you ask me.

'Oh, I dunno,' I said, putting on the groans. 'It's just go, go go. Been up first thing, slaving away over a hot oven, while some folks just loll in bed, easy for them, oh, it's a hard life, being a housewife.'

'Have you pinched them?' said Sez. She was bending down, looking on the floor of the kitchen cupboard, tearing open tins and packets.

'Look, sit down, will you,' I said. 'You better eat this while it's hot, or you'll get thumped. And don't make any mess. Mum says you've got to clear up, so there.'

'Ah, they're here,' said Sez. 'I bet she tried to hide them.'

When I turned round, she was ramming a Double Decker into her mouth, as if it were a race, a Double-Decker-eating race and she'd started late.

'Oh, God,' I said. 'Not before your breakfast.'

'And after,' she said, holding up a Crunchie Bar. 'I bought them with my own money, so belt up and mind your own business.'

'I'm telling Mum,' I said.

'You would, being a little tell-tale baby. Just like you. Go on, tell her, see if I care. This croissant's not hot.'

I looked round for something to throw at her, then I realized how the OW must feel when I go on like that.

'I thought you were going to ration all your gunge from now on,' I said.

'I only have chocolate at weekends,' she said, her mouth full.

'And the rest.'

We're all supposed to be helping Sez, not mocking or criticizing, trying to see she keeps some control over her secret vice and doesn't feel guilty. I've never been a sweet-eater, which is lucky, not since I was seven. I always feel sick so quickly. I do have other vices, some very secret, but we need not go into them.

'Coffee, my petal,' I said. 'And would you like a Mars Bar perhaps, to swill down the Crunchie Bar, hmmm?'

'Get lost. You think you're so clever. If you ate more chocolate, you wouldn't be so spotty.'

'Hold on,' I said. 'I thought it was supposed to be the opposite.'

'Well, look at your spots,' she said, getting up, poking her big fat finger towards a fresh one on my neck, which I was convinced no one could see. 'And you're not supposed to like chocolates. So you say . . .'

'Gerroff,' I said. 'And watch that coffee. You're going to knock it over, though why should I care? You're clearing up.'

'You've got chocolate all wrong,' she said, sitting down again, starting on her Crunchie Bar. 'As usual, you don't understand anything. God knows why they let you in that sixth form. Oh yeah, forgot, they take anyone these days, even with poor O-levels.'

I ignored this dig. Just as I ignored those stupid examiners who had not given me those As I so richly deserved.

'Chocolate is, in fact, very good for you,' she said. 'Do you know there's more calcium in a bar of chocolate than in a hamburger?'

'So what? I don't like hamburgers. And I hate calcium.'

'Liar. You don't even know what calcium is.'

'It's that stuff in your bones, isn't it? Or that stuff you take when you've got the runs . . .'

'Was it a C or a D you got for Science?' said Sez. 'Remind me. No, don't, it's too depressing.'

'Just you wait,' I said. 'Then we'll see how clever you really are.'

'Sugar is also vital for energy,' she said. 'So that would help you. Stop you being so lazy.'

'Thanks.'

'And it's also just been proved that there's more iron in a bar of chocolate than in a raw carrot. So chocolate would give you strength and muscles, stop you being such a weedy, scrawny weakling. Here, catch . . .'

As she marched out of the kitchen, smirking at her own smartness, she threw me her rolled-up ball of chocolate wrappers.

The OF came down just as I was about to leave. I had to be at school by one o'clock if I wanted to set off with the rest of our sixth form. I still hadn't really made up my mind whether to go or not, but what else was there to do, now I was out of work? I wonder if I can go to arbitration. Claim unfair dismissal, bring out all the ice-cream scoopers in the nation.

'Oh, you're still here,' said the OF, smiling. 'I thought you'd be off to work by now.'

'Soon,' I said. I had not yet revealed my humiliation to the world at large, or the world at small, not wanting the subject discussed round the meal table, especially with Sez.

'Does that mean you'll come with me?' he said, rather plaintively.

I was busy clearing away the dishes, and pretended not to hear.

'You haven't been for ever so long. I remember when you

used to plead and plead with me to be taken, then you usually turned out to be a right pain. I remember once you fell asleep on my knee, only to wake up and ask if a corner kick was a goal.'

'Tra-la, tra-la,' I sang. 'No, really, I'd love to come, Dad, but I've promised to go on this march. It is pretty serious. Concerns us all, you know.'

I was trying hard to remember what precisely it was for, apart from being pretty serious. Lots of people were going on it, including lots of our sixth form, including lots of our sixth-form girls, so I'd heard. Not of course that such a thing would affect my decision or cloud my political judgement.

'The Trafalgar Square one?' he asked. I nodded.

I did feel quite nostalgic as I watched him getting ready, going through the old rituals I knew so well. First he made his half-time coffee, putting in hot milk, not cold milk, the way he likes it. We always shared that. You can never get a drink at Spurs at half-time because of all the queues. Before the match we always used to have Bovril, till they changed it to tasteless yucky soup. Then he'd buy me a packet of crisps to keep me going through the match itself.

He got out his duty-free litre bottle of whisky and carefully and slowly decanted the correct measure into his little hip-flask, the one the O W got him as a Christmas present, one of the few he's ever been thrilled by.

And, as usual, it overflowed, spilling all over the kitchen table. All these years and he's never been able to do it properly. I'm surprised the O W hasn't bought him a funnel. As usual, he bent over and licked the pine surface of the table, determined to suck up every last drop of his precious whisky, so nothing was wasted, nothing was lost.

'Hope they win,' I said.

'About time they did,' he said. 'Don't really know why I go.'

'Oh, you love it, admit it.'

He collected together his Thermos and his hip-flask, his pencil to fill in the subs and the half-time scores, his spare gloves and pom-pom hat, the one the O W has tried to hide, as she hates him wearing it so much, but it does keep his bald spot warm. He packed all his stuff in his little designer rucksack and swung it over his right shoulder. And then he set off, a happy little feller.

That rucksack was the second-best Christmas present he's ever had. Sez gave it to him. Wasn't that kind.

Our contingent had to assemble at the school gates, so we'd all been told in a bossy, duplicated leaflet from Sally and the Slags. The term 'slags', never to be used in their presence, refers not to their morals but their fierceness. They really slag you off should you step out of line and make any personal comments about such things as their close-cropped hair and their big boots.

I ran all the way, just in case they had set off without me, in which case I would run straight home and go back to bed till Monday. Look, I might believe in the Cause, but I'm not doing things on my own. I believe in all Causes. You should see the petitions I've signed. It's just getting out of bed that is the real political stumbling-block.

There were only a dozen people there, mostly standing around, smoking, chatting and looking spare, except for Sally and three of her henchpersons who were doing something with the banner, and except for three lower-sixth hicks, admiring Vinny's marching gear. I chose to avoid him.

'Can I give you a hand?' I said to Sal.

'I doubt it,' she said.

'You sound just like my mother,' I said.

'I doubt it,' she said again, spitting. I'd forgotten she'd signed the pledge never to marry, never to have children, never to drink Babycham, never to speak to Tracey.

The banner had previously been used for a Gays and Lesbians March, which, alas, I missed, goodness know what I was doing that day. I could just make out some of the letters, and beneath them were traces of a previous word, Nicaragua, which someone had had a lot of trouble spelling.

We have our own sixth-form banner (doesn't every caring school), very well printed by the Art Department, saying 'BROOKFIELD SIXTH FORM SUPPORTS' at the top, with space below to fill in the appropriate words. We'd had endless discussions on this before deciding we should be positive. There had been a move to say 'BROOKFIELD SIXTH FORM CONDEMNS', or, even simpler and more omni-useful, 'BROOKFIELD SIXTH FORM HATES THATCHER', but both these had been thought too negative.

The trouble is that the words below, usually filled in hurriedly and badly, never look as impressive. After school yesterday someone had just painted in the words THE CUTS, before it was realized they didn't quite go after BROOKFIELD SIXTH FORM SUPPORTS. Sally was busily changing it to say ANTICUTS. It read like a completely new word, sort of a cross between antics and antiques.

'Right. Who's going to start carrying it then?' said Sally, looking round. The banner flapping in the wind and the paint on the new word was still wet. I could see Vinny moving away, not wanting to get his combat gear tarnished. He was all in khaki, dressed for jungle war: a metaphorical statement, of course.

'Where's the rest of the girls?' I said idly, looking around, thinking there was no sign yet of Clarrie or Tracey or other people I thought might turn up, hoped might turn up, mentioning no names.

'Women,' said Sally.

'Where?' I said, thinking she might have spotted some arriving late.

'We are all women, not girls,' said Sally. '"Girls" is a degrading term, just as much as "ladies". Please don't use it again.'

'Sorry, madam,' I said, 'I mean, sorry, woman.'

'What time are the television cameras due?' said Sally, turning to one of her chums.

'Oh, I dunno, Sal. At the Town Hall I think.'

'Okay then,' said Vinny, giving a big sigh. 'Let me take it.'

'And I'll help as well,' I said, grabbing the other end. There was a rush to help, all of us arguing whose turn it would be next.

And so we set off down the road, me and Vinny struggling with the banner, while Sally and the women persons marched behind, all shouting, OUT OUT OUT.

We soon stopped shouting, and soon after that the marching became more like trudging. In the end we just dragged the banner along. We got caught up with the Saturday morning shoppers in the High Road and it all became a bit pathetic; scruffy kids trying to tear our banner, women with trolleys pushing us off the pavement, some Arsenal skinheads offering to fight us.

But when we got to the Town Hall, it was brilliant. There were scores of other schools there, groups from all over the place, some people in costumes and masks, carrying huge colourful banners, waving posters, flying flags. Several contingents had come with their own jazz bands. It was more like a carnival than a march.

'Is this a private party or can anyone join in?'

It was Lol. Lots of our sixth form had decided to join us at the Town Hall rather than school, so our contingent was now pretty large, all of them wanting to hold the banner and do their bit of shouting and yelling. We felt like a football crowd as we roared and cheered.

Some boring Union official got up on a box and addressed us through a megaphone. We couldn't hear a word, but we all cheered like mad. Then a famous politician said a few words, again incomprehensible, and we cheered even louder.

'Where's all the surgeons, then?' said Lol. 'You'd think they'd be here. And the nurses. As we're doing it for them. I only came for the nurses. It's my ambition to have one in uniform.'

'What are you on about?' I said.

'The Cuts. We're protesting against Cuts,' he said, looking at our banner. 'No more vasectomies, that's it, isn't it? Hold on, it's the price of antiques. Of course. I quite agree. Far too expensive these days. UP UP UP UP.'

He staggered around, shouting any old nonsense, making sure that he staggered into the prettiest girls, I mean women, clutching hold of them round the waist to save himself, then not letting go. Someone slapped his face in the end. I recognized her. It was Miss Button, my old primary-school teacher. Never knew she was still alive. You always think they die, once you move on.

By comparison with Lol I felt very committed, genuinely worried about the state of Education and all the things going wrong, the cuts being made, the lack of resources, options being withdrawn, not that I properly understood it all. I used to think that I L E A was some Russian bloke who had disappeared, till Sally put me right.

We all then set off for Whitehall, marching and singing, filling the streets, as the police had stopped the traffic now we were on the official route. There must have been 10,000 of us. It felt terrific as people on the pavements smiled and waved at us, even if most of them were Japanese tourists, very pleased to be capturing some age-old medieval spectacle on their Sony videos. There were lots of people taking photographs, professionals and amateurs, but no sign as yet of the T V cameras.

I suddenly saw Isabella about a hundred yards ahead of me. I gave Lol my end of the banner and tried to work my way forward. There was so much pushing and shoving, people dancing and showing off, waving and shouting, that no matter how much I seemed to push myself forward, I ended up further back. I tried bending down and ducking through the legs, which turned out to be easier. Being weedy and not terribly tall or hefty does have advantages.

She was with a group of other girls, some of whom looked familiar, mainly from our school. She was in a flowing coat I hadn't seen before, but then what do I know about her clothes, what do I know about what she's really like. I felt nervous, rather hot, rather hesitant, as if I were trespassing, yet I'd been on this march from the beginning, a genuine paid-up protester. It would be a natural thing to say hello.

Should I say, excuse me, can I carry your poster? Or, hey, imagine meeting you! Or, how about you and me, baby, demonstrating together? No, too crude.

HONK IF YOU SUPPORT THE TEACHERS.

This huge hand-written poster was stuck in front of me, blinding me completely.

'Whatjafink, Cart,' said Lol. 'Groovy, huh?'

He'd got a supply of blank posters from somewhere and was busy painting slogans on them. PUKE IF YOU LIKE MRS THATCHER. He gave this to an old woman to carry who shoved it up in the air without reading it. TOOT IF YOU HATE THE TORIES. Several were more obscene, instructing the public exactly what to do with themselves, but I won't repeat them. This is a family WP.

It did cause a good deal of audience reaction, especially from lorry drivers and building workers, who all cheered and made appropriate gestures. Lol naturally yelled back at them.

'Don't be so stupid,' I said. 'This is a serious march.'

'Look, rot-guts, what is the main point of all this?'

I ignored him, but he grabbed me by the lapels.

'Listen, fartface, the main object is publicity. To make a public noise, understand? To draw attention to ourselves, so we can draw attention to the cause. Am I right or am I right?'

'But not like that,' I said.

'What a little creep you are. In every sense. Creeping on the ground so you can look up girls' knickers. I know your sort. WATCH OUT GIRLS. There's a dirty young man around. HE'S CALLED CARTNER . . .'

I saw a gap ahead and managed to get in, determined to get away from Lol. Nobody could really hear him with all the noise, but I didn't want him around being lewd and crude when I talked to Isabella.

I was catapulted forward like a missile, far quicker than I wanted to be, then I was propelled from side to side like a pin-ball machine, and I began to feel quite dizzy, losing my sense of direction. When the next wave pushed me forward, I couldn't stop myself and I fell right against Isabella's back. Only it wasn't Isabella.

'Do you mind,' said Sez, turning round and glaring at me. Had I lost Isabella? Had I never even seen her? Had it been Sez all along? She was still in her dressing-gown thing, that stupid garment she had worn at breakfast.

'Oh, it's you,' she said.

'Have you seen, er . . .' I hesitated, not wanting to give anything away, such as my stupidity. 'Er Downing Street. Any sign of it yet?'

'We're not allowed in there, stupid,' she said. 'You know it's been barricaded off for years. How many marches have you been on?'

'Lots, clever clogs, most of them before you were born.'

'Why aren't you doing something really socially useful, such as watching Spurs?'

'Ha, ha,' I said.

'Or manning the ice-cream scoops. Shouldn't you be at work anyway?'

She moved sideways, leaving room for me to get in beside her and her friends. I knew she was just being horrible because it was me. With your friends, that's how you behave. One must not appear soppy or show any of that brotherly love nonsense. I realize that having a brother in the sixth form is socially quite acceptable if you're in the fourth, but I certainly didn't want to walk with her. I'd have more of Lol's crass comments to put up with.

'I was just wondering where the rest of the sixth-form girls were,' I said, looking round, hoping still to spot Isabella.

'Women,' said Sez.

Oh no, not that one again. Don't say it's reached the fourth year as well.

'See yous anyway,' I said. 'The Prime Minister wants a private word with me, so I'd better split.'

I edged my way out of the marching columns. We were just going round Trafalgar Square at the time. I was exhausted anyway, what with all that walking, all that carrying the banner and me not being very strong. I should have asked Sez for a bar of chocolate. She usually has emergency supplies hidden somewhere on her person.

My feet were killing me. I think my reserve trainers had had it, as I could feel every cobble, every paving stone. I took them off, bathed my feet in the fountain and then lay down beside the lions to have a rest. How was I going to get home? I'd come out with no money. I found I was still holding a poster, shoved into my hand at some time. SCREAM IF YOU LOVE SPURS it said. At least that was fairly harmless. On the other side it said STRIP OFF IF YOU FANCY ME. Very Lol.

'I thought it was you,' said a voice. 'Get on.'

I was still lying on my back. Above me a figure in a motorbike helmet was leaning over. It seemed like a space-man at first, from out of the heavens, as all I could see was sky.

'I recognized your banal poster right away. Look, do you want a lift home or not?'

I got up and climbed on the back of the bike. Quite a large one, the usual Japanese sort, big enough to take a whole family, never mind two sixth-formers. I looked for the L-plate, which I'd noticed on it when it was parked outside school only last week for everyone to admire.

'Passed your test then,' I yelled, as we roared off. I got no reply. Probably just thrown the L-plate away. I hoped the police didn't see us, but they probably had better things to do, stopping the marchers getting into Downing Street.

We went faster once we were heading north, along Tottenham Court Road, and I had to hold on tight, bending my body so that it fitted in with the body in front, making the same shape as I held on to her.

It was rather exciting. Sensuous, even, swaying with her body, moving as one, or trying to, because she swerved in and out of the traffic, racing cars at all the lights, going on the pavement if the way ahead was blocked.

'Bloody women drivers,' I shouted in her left ear. Then I smiled at what I'd just said. By chance rather than intention I hadn't used the word 'girls'. That was fortunate.

'Cheers, Sal,' I said as I got off, hobbling rather, but putting it on, staggering around with my legs apart like a drunken cowboy.

'A pleasure,' she said. What a pretty smile, sorry, better take back the word 'pretty'. What an attractive smile. And such nice teeth. Can I use the word 'nice'? Why not. It's not sexist. Oh, what the hell. In school Sally always seems to scowl so much these days, but it's probably a performance, just as Vinny poses, Tracey screeches, Clarrie says 'super' and Lol is lewd. What about me? Oh, I'm just lovely all the time, but then that is natural to me, with no pretence.

'Where was your bike then?' I asked. Sally was taking off her helmet and locking it to a carrier thing on the back, all very efficient and organized.

'I took it down last night and left it locked, as I knew I'd need it today.'

'Hey, where's this?' I said, looking around. She had said she'd take me home.

'Our squat. Come on in and have some coffee.'

She banged three times on a boarded-up door. The house looked completely derelict, all the windows barricaded, waiting for the demolition gang to finish it off. A window opened high up and a bunch of keys fell down on the end of a string. She opened a padlock on the front door and the keys disappeared up in the air.

'Nice little place you've got here,' I said as we stepped over some piles of old mattresses, ducked through a large hole in a wall, climbed over broken furniture then up some stairs, which were missing their banisters and most of the steps.

'How long you been here, Sal?'

'Since I left home,' she said. 'Correction. Since I got chucked out of home.'

She led me into her room, which was better than I expected, quite artistic and cleaner than the rest of the house. The furniture was all bashed up, straight from some skip, as were the ornaments, but I could see her school books on a shelf, all very tidy. In a corner was a mattress on the floor. A double mattress, I noted. Did she live alone. Did she sleep alone.

She took off her heavy jacket, which immediately made her look far less manly. Then she unfastened some straps and her trousers fell down, that is, her thick, heavy-duty army surplus overalls fell down. She was now in some boxer shorts, men's variety but very revealing, and a skimpy CND T-shirt. She kicked her overalls into a corner, switched on a gas fire and then filled a kettle for coffee.

'What about crumpets?' she asked. 'I think we have some somewhere, if they're not mouldy. You can toast them. Make yourself useful.'

'Oh, I'm always useful,' I said. 'I made the breakfast for the whole family this morning.'

'So?' she said, glaring at me. 'Don't you do that every morning?'

Oh no, don't say it's going to get heavy, just when I was thinking whatever it was I was beginning to think. Thoughts of Isabella had gone completely. I probably never saw her today. Probably never see her again.

'You eat the food, don't you? You should therefore take an equal share in the provisioning, preparing, cooking and cleaning up.'

It was nice to be sitting and having a decent conversation, communing, sharing life, chewing the cud with someone who wasn't stupid. Tracey and Marie had not exactly called for a lot of intellectual effort.

'Very true, O wise one,' I said.

I could have been risking my neck here, had I put a foot wrong or made some really silly remark, so I had to take care. I've always preferred clever women. But what I don't know is, do they prefer me?

'I do contribute in other ways,' I said. 'Each to our strengths. One helps the common good according to what one can do best. Only wish I knew what my strengths were. If any.'

'The main reason I left home was because I could no longer take responsibility for my parents.'

'I know how you feel,' I said, wondering how she felt.

'There's something I want you to do for me,' she said, suddenly all smiles.

'If it's my body you're after,' I said, 'it's spoken for. I promised the Medical Research Council that they could have it, in virgin condition, one careful owner, hardly used, only a handful of miles on the clock – well, I do live very near school.'

'Your body could be useful,' she said, studying me. 'I have no prejudices. It's the rest of the world that is prejudiced. I am open to all experiences, all sensations. Are you?'

'Bien sure,' I said. 'Count me in.'

'You're counted,' she said, lighting a cigarette. Huh, and I thought she would be a non-smoking, non-swearing, non-violent vegan. How life surprises one.

'You're not a nihilist, are you?' I said. 'Always wanted to meet one of those. Or an anarchist. Or a structuralist. They sound really weird. We're C of E in our house, except at supper-times when they all become veggies.'

She was watching me very carefully, crossing and recrossing her legs, smiling to herself, then she lay back on the cushions, and blew a smoke ring, stretching her arms and legs as if doing exercises.

'All right then,' I said. 'I can perhaps afford to abuse this body, just once. But don't tell anyone.'

'I was wondering when you would,' she said. 'You must be almost eighteen by now.'

'Any minute now, duckie,' I said. 'You'll see it in *The Times*, don't worry. On the Court Pages.'

'Can't wait,' she said, stretching even more.

'I never promised them that my body would be totally unadulterated, unsullied by contact with any foreign bodies,' I said, putting on my best Lol-ish leer.

'That's good,' she said.

'Come on then, lass. Where's these crumpets you've been boasting about? I will have one after all.'

She waved a hand to a plastic carrier bag in the corner. I

got out a packet of crumpets and toasted two, one for each of us. I know my place, even if I don't know what's going on, in life or anywhere else. Especially not here. I felt as if I were caught in some game without having been told the rules.

'So what is it you want to do to me, I mean, me to do for you?' I said, butter running down my chin. No, I tell a lie. Flora margarine. She got off the bed and immediately assumed her businesslike and bossy face, which is how she usually looks at school.

'We've done this amazing petition, as you know, 'cos you signed it. Everyone did.'

'Remind me. Hey, are these Waitrose's or Sainsbury's? Not bad. Must tell my Mum to get them. I mean, splurge splurge, I must buy some for my mother, next time I'm provisioning . . .'

'The End of Examinations Petition. We want them stopped at once, as all they do is breed people who are good at exams, which is of no use to the world at all. And we want our school, unilaterally, to set an example to the rest of London, the rest of the world . . .'

'Oh, that one, yeah, I did sign it.'

'We've decided you are the best person to present it to the Head.'

'Why me?'

'You're sort of nondescript, non-party, anonymous really . . .'

'Oh, thanks a lot,' I said. 'Wish I'd stayed on the pavement in Trafalgar Square.

'And you also appear to be, God knows why, rather popular.'

'Now you're getting closer,' I said. 'And so am I.' I went over to her, just to see what she would do, how she would react. I'd decided to get to the bottom of all this teasing, or the top. 'Okay, I will then,' I said. 'But what are you going

74

to do for me?' I stood waiting, licking my lips as clean as possible. I hate this polyunsaturated rubbish. Give me good poisonous butter any time.

There was a soft tap at the door. It opened, and in came Mr Barnes.

I practically swallowed my last mouthful of crumpet. What was he doing here? Could he have left his horrible wife and begun living in a squat? Could there be something going on between him and Sally? All those attacks she was always making on him must be just a cover. What was going on?

'God, is it that time?' said Sally, jumping up. 'I forgot.' She took down some books from a shelf and handed Barnes what looked like an essay. She had already forgotten my presence. Old Barnes settled down to read, also ignoring me, very much at home, as if this were a regular arrangement, whatever the arrangement was. Extra lessons of some sort, presumably. Lots of people, mostly in a panic, have now got private tutors. But I was amazed at Sally. Perhaps it's for S-levels, as she is the only one in our class taking them, or some more private kind of lesson.

'See you then,' I said. 'Gotta go. Starving family at home and I've got to feed them. I do have responsibilities. Bye.'

They didn't even look at me. I let myself out of the house and walked home, straight to my little room and my little friend.

Just take it easy, Cartner, don't let it worry your simple mind. Yes, it is all very confusing. But you are very young and immature for your age. Just tell yourself that you got out of your depth, out of your field, and from now on do try to stick to what you know and understand.

Thanks, WP. Good advice. Nice to know I do have one real friend in the world.

6 A High Old Time with some Terribly Nice People

I have this girl who keeps ringing me. Oh, you know how it is, pursued from pillar-box to post-box. Really I should have a social secretary to keep my affairs in order, order my affairs, take my orders, mix my affairs. Twice this week I've come home and Sez has told me this girl has been after me. They all are, darling, that's the way it goes if you're the hunkiest brute in the sixth form.

'She sounds old,' said Sez.

Oh no, I'm not in, I've gone out for a few years, I'm in conference till the year 2000.

'And she sounds posh.'

Hmm, that could be more interesting. So who could it be? I haven't been out in the wide world for five weeks now, not what you'd call out, and it's almost Easter and almost time for the exams and almost time for my pension book and senior citizen's bus pass. Did a whole life whizz past without my noticing? So it goes. Gone.

Just like my job. That's why for the last five weeks I've been here, in my room, my cage, my prison, sitting in front of my user-friendly WP, hello Cart, how ya doin, how's trix. God, my knees are hurting. It's with typing on this stupid screen. I must be sitting in a stupid way, or this chair is at the wrong height, or the table is wonky, or it's my knees going, going, gone. I'll never need that bus pass at this rate.

'Ring, ring.'

That's the phone. Yup, you're right. We have one outside on the landing now, how smart, how modern and how totally unfair. Another example of how that girl is completely spoiled. When I was her age, tra-la, I had nothing. Now she gets anything she wants. Going out late tonight, dear, bingo, here you are darling, the taxi fare home. Just 'cos she's a girl. Oh, some new clothes, quick, take this sack full of pound notes and just you nip down to Oxford Street and buy a few shops. Pocket-money, at once, my petal, just open your pocket and I'll shove it all in. Now she's got her very own telephone extension. I know, it's for both of us, that's the theory, but do I get on it? Do I heck. Who rings me anyway, when do I ever go out etc.

It is true to say of teenage girls, as I have found from my enormous experience of them at close quarters (all one of them, this slut to whom I'm supposedly related), that they live their lives on the phone.

I've seen Sez come home, wave fond farewells to her best friend Fez at the gate, even give her a kiss (they've all gone potty these days, I blame those feminists), then rush up the stairs, reach the top just as the phone rings, drag it screaming

77

into her room and throw her enormous body on her bed; then for the next forty minutes all I hear is her laughing and roaring, loud and raucous and totally artificial, like some paid fool from the Wogan audience. And guess what? It will be Fez on the line. The stupid girl she's just left ten seconds ago and has been with all day long anyway.

'Cartner! It's for you,' shouted Sez.

Must be a wrong number, or Lol wanting to borrow my essay again, or Silas, stuck for once in his life and needing to ask me how to spell Porlock.

You know and I know, and I know you know. From the first moment I was told that some new girl was ringing me, a voice no one recognized, my little tired old heart had been singing a little song all to itself, oh, Isabella, strange fits of passion have I known. Hey, that sounds familiar. Don't say some of that rubbish has sunk in. I could well get my B after all.

'Hurry up,' yelled Sez again, most unladylike. 'I need that bloody phone. I'm expecting vital messages.'

'Get lost,' I said. 'And I'm telling Mum you swore. I'll probably be on for a very long time. I'd leave home if I were you and move into a phone-box. Come on, give me the rotten thing. I'm not answering it in here, not with you listening, I have no privacy in this house anyway . . .'

I tripped over the wire trying to get it loose, then I fell over some of her stupid busts and ornaments and got lost in her maze of cushions and pillows and mattresses. She has no bed now, how terribly trendy, or drawers or cupboards. It's all al fresco, don't you know, living on the run, letting it all hang out.

I finally dragged the phone to the landing and banged Sez's bedroom door closed. I pulled the phone into my room and managed to get about six inches of the line on to my own bed, where I could pretend I was alone in the whole world, with just my long lost, long lust, love-heart about to breathe nice things in my ear.

'Hi.'

She did have a nice voice. I'd never properly listened to it before, disembowelled, or is it disembodied?

'Hi,' I said, not knowing what to say, or even grunt, in reply.

Good conversation, huh. I hope that beggar Sez is not listening on the downstairs phone. She'll think we've finished, call that a phone call, and will start dialling her dopey friends.

'Sorry, just lost something.' I could hear pages being turned.

'That's all right,' I said. 'I often lose things myself, like my way, my name, my number, the secret of the universe, those sorts of humdrum thing.'

'Cartner,' she said, no longer distracted, all jolly and sexy. I suppose while I'd kept her waiting, thinking of what to say, she'd gone off and written an essay, or got out her phone book and was looking up better blokes to ring.

'Can you come to a dinner party tomorrow night, please say you can, it'll be super if you can, sorry it's short notice, but, har, har.'

I was beginning to recognize those dulcet tones. Clarrie, our sixth form's answer to Princess Di. In the third year, which was when she came into the school, probably from some Swiss finishing school, she'd had the piss taken something rotten, but she'd survived, accent and bubbly personality and genuine niceness intact; and now in the sixth form, amongst the pretend human beings, the almost civilized cream, she'd emerged as our tame Sloane, leader of a small group of like-minded, awfully decent girls. How do they manage it? Answer: it's an Inner London sixth form of 600, or is it 6,000? I've never counted. We've probably got members of the Royal Family or the Dalai Lama or Lord Lucan lurking in some cupboard on the top floor, unknown and unseen because no one's ever talked to them. You have to stand up and shout and wave. Or you drown, anonymously.

'Hold on,' I said, 'I'll get my Filofax out, see if the Moon's in Aquarius, check the balance on my Lloyds Cashcard, ENTER the Amstrad to see what my leader, the PCW 9512, commands to me to do tomorrow night . . . No, you're in luck. I'm free.'

'What about your job? They won't make you work late, will they?'

It's still a secret, about getting the sack. All the same, curious that she even knew I had a job. Had I ever slipped her a free scoop? Had she been told by someone? Hmm, interesting.

'Oh, you mean my Saturday job. Yeah, I've moved on to the Savoy, but I think they'll manage without me this week. The *maître d'hôtel* owes me a few favours anyway.'

'Oh that's super, eight o'clock sharp.'

'I'm always sharp, that's why I bleed all the time, cutting myself to the quick . . .'

But she'd gone, hung up in a hurry to ring round a few more chums. I wonder who I'm replacing? Who has let her down? And anyway, what's her address?

I think I went there once in the fifth year, the last afternoon after O-levels. We had jelly and custard, terribly witty, but I can't remember where it was. Oh well, that's Saturday filled, back to the grind. I wonder who else will be there? Back to that essay.

I wonder if She, you-know-who, is one of her friends. It could have been her who told Clarrie where I worked. Used to work. Will she be there? Oh, the reveries I'll squeeze out of this.

An hour later. Goodness, I haven't left a gap on the screen.

The world will never know there was a long, boring pause there, in my short, boring life.

A beautifully embossed card has just been pushed through our front letter-box. Clarrie does know how to do things in style, what, what. I've now learned two things. Her name is Clarissa. How did I ever not know that? Just never struck me. She probably kept it quiet deliberately. The other fact, oh, shock horror, is in the bottom left-hand corner of the stupid card: BLACK TIE.

'Dad, where are you, I want you. What does this mean, Mum? Get out of my way, Sarah, you peasant.'

And so it came to pass, Saturday night, all right, yah, oh I say, chaps, is it Manuel from Fawlty Towers or the Twit of the Year Award? Mum was thrilled. She was following me round the house with her Olympus Trip, which she still doesn't seem to be able to work properly.

I hate having my photo taken. It's all so fake and formal, stiff and starched. No, it's more than that. I suspect that they are trying to steal something from me, creep into my soul, enter my inner thoughts and then sneak out samples to hold against me for ever. It isn't really me anyway, just some stranger masquerading, wearing my skin. If they'd just take the photie quick, on the run when you're not looking, that wouldn't be so bad, but they insist on full-frontal, family line-ups, oh, Grandma is going to love this, just one more, please, Cartner, can't you smile for once? Must you have that scowl on every photograph?

We couldn't find cuff-links, whatever they are. The Old Feller has not worn his monkey suit for fifteen years and can't remember where he put them. The Old Biddy even went into her secret drawer where she keeps her own copy of the A–Z, one we are not even allowed to know exists, as she says we eat them, and got out her own roll of Sellotape, which she keeps hidden for the same reasons, what a pig she can be. She tried sticking my cuffs together, as she was so desperate to have me dolled up in this stupid suit, but they came to pieces again. In the end, Sez made them stay together by using a stapler, which she had hidden in her room. What a house. No one trusts anyone. But rather clever, using a stapler, so we all thought. Sisters do have their uses, few though they are.

It was hard walking to Clarrie's, the actual act of walking, one step in front of the other. These bloody Sixties trousers of my dad's are so narrow. Getting them on was hell, like pulling on a wet-suit, which I haven't done either, but getting them off will be heller. What if I need to get them off in a hurry because, oh, I dunno, some beautiful blonde – I mean, some dark-haired girl with a Spanish name – is just panting for me? Oh, all is fantasy. It won't be that sort of party. Clarissa's father will probably be there, butling. The vicar will say grace.

And this bloody bow-tie is killing my Adam's apple. I never used to have one, but this last year I've felt it grow. Can't think of the reason why, not going anywhere, not doing anything, just a pointless appendage, like another I could mention. God did make a mess of so many things, which some of us, it turns out, alas and alack, don't need.

My dad had put it on for me. He was just as bad, just as soppy, fussing over me as I was getting ready, coming out with all his stupid memories of the Sixties when he was a student and went to Hops, whatever they are. I caught him out though. He usually boasts that he was marching and demonstrating all through the Sixties in his afghan jacket and sandals, so how come he had time for Hops? Always knew it was a lie, typical of *Independent* readers.

I could not have put the tie on by myself as I have never, repeat never, tied a tie in my life. It's my ambition to keep it that way. It was hard in the first year, as we still had school uniform and we had to have a tie, but there was no rule that said you had to wear it, I sussed that out right away, but it meant I had to keep one in my pocket, just in case some sod got clever. I was in the second year when all uniform was abolished. End of story.

Oh, there was that time Mrs Thatcher – remember her? Prime Minister or something – came to our school to present something or other, and if you were in a class the old bat might walk into, you had to have the school tie on all day. But my mum tied it for me, so I've kept up my vow. My dad says if I get any university interviews (and that reminds me, what the hell are they playing at? Never did trust that postman, not since I found out he was an Arsenal fan), then I'll need to wear a tie and a jacket. Hard Cheddar. If that's a condition for university, I'll stay at home.

I'd forgotten that Clarrie lived in a block of flats, but they are rather big and private-looking, and it's not far from Regent's Park. Must be a nice class of con-merchant lives round here. Would Isabella already be inside? Would she have a Black Tie? And anything else? That could be interesting. All the girls naked, except for little black ties over their – well, they don't have Adam's apples, at least, not in the photos I've seen.

No lift. Total silence down well-carpeted corridors and dark, panelled wooden walls, then inside, another intercom thing and a security peep-hole in every front door.

Clarrie's flat was enormous, with doors, chandeliers and Indian carpets everywhere. A girl called Deborah had just arrived ahead of me, she's in my History group, but I don't talk to her. She was handing over some present and they were kissing each other like long-lost sisters and saying, Happy Birthday, darling. I didn't know. Nobody had told me. I would have brought some well-chosen, rather expensive, rather imaginative present, if only I'd known, tra-la-la, and other unlikely stories . . .

Lol and Silas were already there. And Vinny. Oh no, not him, I might as well pack up now. He has this knack of making me feel inferior. Lol, for all his knowledge of the world and its women, does not have that effect, nor does Silas, our Boy Wonder, nice to see them both there. But Vinny says very little, does very little and still inhibits me. He's always done it, makes me feel neolithic.

In the first year, while I was 'flying up' from the Cubs, and was quite excited for a week to be in the Boy Scouts before I quickly realized my mistake, Vinny had a part in *Grange Hill*. You must have seen him. Everybody saw him. On the second-year school camp, when we went to that awful place in Wales, Vinny turned up in a Che Guevara hat and sunglasses, which he never took off. My concern in life at the time was collecting those Esso, or was it Shell, football badges. The next year he wore black for the whole year, in memory of Lennon. I was too busy filling in my World Cup chart to take much notice.

The year after, we all took a lot of notice as Vinny began the autumn term by glue-sniffing, then moved on to magic mushrooms, those things you pick up on the Heath. I did try it once, bunking off Maths with Lol, but it knackered my back, bending over, and wore out my eyes, and we didn't find anything.

Then Vinny had a lost year, said to be due to LSD and another lost year when he ended up in some boarding-school, council-run so he says, but that could have been a cover for Borstal or prison, or Eton. You don't ask Vinny these things. He just stands around, grunting, glottal-stopping his way through a few expletives, all in a thick, North London accent.

As you might have guessed, he's pure posho. His Dad, last seen by him the day he was born, is a Labour MP and his Mum is a Hon. I don't hate him just for those reasons but because he's already had articles printed in some trendy glossy mags on what make-up London teenagers are wearing today, makes you sick, and he's got a job lined up at LWT, that's if he doesn't go to Oxford, which his Dad can fix for him.

'Look at this,' I shouted suddenly, 'I'm bleeding.' Can envy and jealousy make you do that? By the pricking of my thumbs, something Vinny this way comes. A stigmata, that's it. 'I've just been standing here, doing nothing,' I said, 'yet there's blood pouring out of my arms. Wait till they hear about this in Lourdes. I could be huge. People could pay a fortune to touch me. I could be a saint, a holy personage, the new St Bob Geldof.'

People did stop and listen for a few moments. I was honestly completely perplexed by what had happened. My hands had touched nothing, been nowhere. Vinny came across, looked at me, then slowly rolled up my sleeves. The metal staples on my cuffs had come loose and had scratched my wrists, enough to draw thin trickles of blood.

'I'll make an excuse and go now, where's me coat and top hat, hand me my walking-stick, James.'

I walked off, furious, into the next room. It was a formal dining room, with a polished table and candles about to be lit. I noticed place names all down the table; quick as a flash I was round them, not looking for moi, where is it, Is, Isa, Isab . . .

'Oh, you naughty boy,' said Clarrie, 'you're not supposed to be here, not just yet, come with me, my special birthday cake is almost ready.'

She took me into the kitchen, big enough to cater for the QE2, where two of her Sloaney friends, neither from our school, were fussing and shrieking in front of a space-age, electronic wall-oven. They were both in low-cut tulle creations, cocktail dresses I suppose they're called, or crinolines, search me, which rattled and crumpled. I wondered what effect a microwave would have on them, would they heat, or disintegrate, or just say 'pass'. How do they manage to keep them on the edges of their shoulders, just above the nipples? Wires, I expect, or years of special breathing exercises.

They ushered me out again, saying I mustn't look, it wasn't quite ready. I could see no sign of parents in the kitchen, so that was something, nor any ancient retainers, or Filipino slaves. Les gels were doing all the catering themselves, gosh, what spiffing fun.

'I say, be a darling, Cartner, and open the champagne, I think most people are here by now.'

It really was champagne, my first sup. Horrible, yuck, give me Foster's any time. Naturally I had to give it a reasonable try after all the PR it's had and the fame that surrounds it. I did the same with Shakespeare, gave him the benefit of the doubt so no one could call me hasty or prejudiced, before deciding he writes a load of old cobblers, corny clichés that he just happened to come out with first. He doesn't even have any opinions, always giving you every side, how boring, so you never know what he believes, what he really thinks. Barnes refuses to listen when I go on like this, calling me obtuse, must look that up some time, and infantile. Let's hope I always stay infantile. Better than being conned and pretending not to be.

'So what happened at Cambridge, Silas old son?' said Lol, as I passed round the champagne. This was news to me. I didn't know he'd tried. Even Vinny was interested.

'You'll be trying to get into Queens', I suppose,' said Lol, making a disgusting gesture with a champagne bottle. The women were in the kitchen making their magic, while we chaps chatted. Not that their presence would have inhibited Lol.

'King's, actually,' said Silas.

'What did happen?' said Vinny.

'Hey, you've got a speaking part at last,' said Lol, going

86

behind Vinny and pretending to pull strings in his back like a puppet. 'He's not just a beautiful spy after all. Hey, are you wearing a truss?'

'Piss off,' said Vinny, quietly but meaning it. They were such opposites, Lol and Vinny, one all loud and brash, the other cool and silent, but equally smart movers when there was talent around.

'Hey, you guys,' I said. 'Calm down. This is a birthday party, remember.'

'Well, if the piss is off, I'll have more champagne.'

'It was really rather boring,' said Silas. 'One of the tutors asked me what I had in my carrier bag, so I had to get everything out.'

'Good job nobody asked you, Vin,' said Lol. 'It would be either your make-up or stolen goods from Woolies.'

Everyone ignored Lol this time. He was trying too hard.

'I had the latest 2000 AD, which I'd read on the train,' said Silas. 'A copy of *Cycling News* and, by chance, I did have one history book, some old Taylor I think.'

'All well worked out, eh Silas, you sly old poseur,' said Lol.

'And have you heard?' asked Vinny.

'This morning. Conditional offer. I just have to get two Es.'

We all cheered at this. He'd kept it all so quiet, which was the best thing to do. Amazing really, with his background, but he does happen to be brilliant at every lesson, lucky sod. He's doing five A-levels, including Latin in his own time, as the syllabus can't fit it in. There's one in every school. Makes you sick.

'Eeees-ee, eees-ee,' shouted Lol, swaying and punching the air like a football supporter.

'None of my places have offered me anything yet,' I said. 'I blame that sod Barnes. I bet he gave me a really bad prediction.'

'Just because you're looooz-ing,' sang Lol.

'I don't really feel envious of you, Silas,' I said, feeling the champagne beginning to flow. 'Being a brain-box is a curse, if you ask me.'

'No one asked you,' said Lol.

'Cleverness is a handicap, not an asset,' I said. 'You've always got to demonstrate it. For the rest of your life, anything less than an A will be a failure. And eventually it will happen. The higher you go, the smaller the top will become. It's like a pyramid. In the end there's only room for one at a time. You're on a conveyor belt, and it's bound to lead to disappointment and heartbreak. Stay on the slopes with us, Si, much more room, much more enjoyment. Yes, I will have some more champagne, thanks Vin.'

'What's he on about?' said Lol. 'I think he's wandering. First he's climbing a pyramid, then on a conveyor belt, next he's on some slope. I think you need extra lessons from Barnes, old son, or a brain transplant.'

I took a swing at Lol, a pretend swing, just wanting to push him away, make him belt up, but I slipped and fell on the floor, so they all laughed, ha ha ha.

'I think you have a point,' said a familiar voice, with a familiar comment. It was Isabella, smiling at me. I hadn't heard her come in.

'All you are doing,' said Silas, 'is rationalizing your own lack of academic success, explaining it away, excusing yourself because you know you can and should do better. You think that your specious argument, therefore, gets you out of trying.'

'You have a point there, too, Silas,' said Isabella. 'And you didn't slur your speech.'

'Hey, whose side are you on?' I said.

'Actually,' said Lol, 'I think you're a load of plonkers. I'm fed up with this chat. I miss those parties where we took everything out of the fridge and threw it at the walls. That was real intellectual stuff.'

Vinny was now back to saying nothing, just standing around, looking superior and bored. He was all in white, an immaculate white jacket like a band leader's and what could have been cricket trousers, but with the required little black tie. Silas also had a white jacket on, which in his case was very dramatic. All the girls had complimented them on their gear. No one had mentioned my suit. The collar was killing me, and my cuffs. I wished I'd come in jeans.

Vinny gave one of his bored sighs, pushed back his floppy hair, then pushed off round the room, giving us all the benefit of his other profile. Then it struck me that he was not, in fact, admiring himself for once. He was manoeuvring nearer Isabella. Bloody hell.

She was deep in the same boring conversation with Silas, the one I'd begun but grown tired of. She seemed very struck by his argument, and by him. Not another. I could have two rivals, two opponents to knock out, even before anyone had realized I was in the running. Isabella herself had seemed oblivious so far of my commanding presence and powerful intellect and incredible wit. I could feel myself going all sullen and silent, moody and withdrawn, the world does not understand me, hey ho. Isabella, why don't you smile at me personally, let me know, just a little sign? I could end up this evening really bitter and twisted, then I'll never have a chance.

The cake was brought in with great excitement. Lol did some fanfares with his mouth, well, he is musical, plus a few belches and farts to show he wasn't phased by all this upper-sixth Sloaney intellectual crap. The girls roared and cheered.

We all sang 'Happy Birthday', and Clarrie cut the cake and gave us each a bit. It was delicious, hot and steaming from the oven, very light, a sort of coffee-and-spice taste, just the way I like it. It's supposed to give you a sore tum, so my mum always says, eating cake so hot, but then mums are hired to say that.

'Yes, if you're offering, Clarrie old gel,' I said. 'Just another. A soupçon.'

'There is smoked salmon to come,' she said, 'and then *boeuf bourgignon*, so don't fill yourself up.'

But I insisted, being a good guest. No one else had seconds or thirds, and they all stared at me, some of them giggling and whispering. I don't mind being considered a pig.

That was when I had to sit down. I'd already had quite a bit of the champagne, trying it out for taste, and had begun to feel terribly happy. But the cake had suddenly made me strangely dizzy and confused, and knocked out, not all here. High, perhaps. Oh no.

I had simply never realized it. I'm not used to these upper-class parties. Cannabis cake. Of course. Everyone must have known it was coming, except me. Too much of a hick, too busy keeping an eye on Vinny and Silas, too busy guzzling, too busy showing off with my boring theories. And they just let me be greedy, the rotten sods.

They put me to rest for a bit in another room, with the light off. After about an hour I did feel much better. When I emerged, the smoked salmon had all been finished, but I did get some of the *boeuf bourgignon*. They wouldn't let me touch the wine, which was just as well, considering how I hammered that champagne, complaining all the time that I still didn't like it.

If I try hard, I can remember bits of what happened after that. I could hear people screaming and yelling their thanks, triffic, wonderful, fab, bono, super, darling, thanks awfully for having us. I felt very warm towards all of them, towards the whole world. Perhaps I'll stay high for ever. I like it there.

I like it here as well. Exactly where I am now, where I've ended up, the situation I now find myself in, as of this moment in the millennium. I can hardly believe it.

Isabella brought me home. There, that surprised you. I

don't think I've ever taken a girl to her home before much less been taken home myself. They always make an excuse and say they have to go with a friend, or their Dad's picking them up. What a way to begin a relationship. Life. This must be it. Oh, come on, I can't be imagining everything.

I do recall holding on to her, her taking my hand, her leading me through the streets. Before we got inside my house, just on the doorstep, she gave me a kiss. Surely I can't have made that up. She told me on the doorstep that I'd talked non-stop all the way home, most of it nonsense. I think I do remember that. Then she came in, made sure I got upstairs, rang for a cab and went home.

Promising to see me tomorrow. She did. Truly.

I've just awakened, still the middle of the night, but just had to tell you, get it down before it fades, gets wiped away, or some other rotters play another silly trick on me. They can't, ha ha. I know it, I feel it, it's happened.

Hold on. Here's her phone number and what time to ring her, written down in her own fair hand, so saying, so sighing, clutching his little scrap, our hero fell into another sleep, his head just missing the EXIT button, perchance to wake, perchance to dream, perchance to begin his Real Life at long, long last . . .

7 Bliss and Brighton

This won't take long. The last two weeks have gone in a flash and have lasted two million years, all of which I can describe also in a flash. I've done so much work as well, which is surprising. I thought I'd be lost to humanity, unable to concentrate, or settle, or do anything else except mope: that's what the songs say. So does *Smash Hits*. Probably Shakespeare as well. They all say much the same.

I have begun to raise my expectations above Kentish Town Poly, although there's nothing wrong with it, I'd be well pleased to go there, and am now beginning to think I could slip into Sussex, disguised, of course, as a Sloane. That is the only worry. Clarrie and les gels are trying for places there, which is a right turn-off, but the turn-on is the fact that your friend and mine is also trying, the light of what I thought was my declining life, the one and only, tar-ran-ta-ta, Isabella.

Turns out she's not the only one. We met another Isabella yesterday in Brighton.

We went there, *à deux*, what a day it was, what a night, phew, it really was, such a fright. We walked along the whole front holding hands. Fast, huh, what a mover, Speedy Gonzales watch out, you're nothing but a slowcoach, nothing but a hound dog, tra-la.

What a lot of singing I've been doing recently, what a lot of sentimental old rubbishy songs have come into my head. If only WPs could sing, could pick up the tune instead of just the words. Bound to happen. It was silent films for decades until talkies came in. The next generation of software is bound to be able to talk and sing it all back to you. Perhaps I should concentrate on perfecting such a machine. Haven't invented anything for ages. I was always doing that at one time, lying in my pit, watching the patterns in the ceiling cracks, thinking of schemes and plots to make myself an instant millionaire. I could do with the dosh now. Wasn't cheap, that cheap-day student rail-ticket to Brighton. Especially now that I'm unemployed. Sez wouldn't lend me anything, mean thing.

Isabella paid her own way, of course. She can carry me if she wants, open all doors, stand up for me on any crowded tube or bus. We're all equal now, every sex. This is the modern age.

Yet those people over there, and that lot, look, back over the hill, they must have believed they, too, were in the modern age. There must have been a modern age in the caves, compared with an olden age in the caves. How weird, how strange, yet how comforting. It's about the only thing humanity can look forward to, that we can claim for ourselves, feel pretty damn smart about. WE ARE ALWAYS THE MODERN AGE. There must be a song lurking there.

*

The Sussex wind was like a scythe, the cold pierced my skull, the rain soaked my chromosomes, and was I down-hearted.

I moaned all the time.

'You haven't stopped complaining since we left London,' she said.

'That's the way I like it,' I said. 'Never happier than when I'm having a good moan.'

'Or having someone to blame,' said Isabella, smiling. 'That's what your mother said yesterday.'

'What? You been spying on me?'

'She told me that yesterday.'

Isabella had called for me at home, and I'd had to leave her in the hall for only a minute to get a scarf, but while my back was turned, the Old Bat must have got at her.

'I bet she was hiding in the sitting-room, waiting to pounce on you,' I said.

'She seemed rather nice,' said Isabella. 'Asked me lots of questions.'

'Oh, God. I thought I told you not to talk to strange women. Or strange men.'

'You're pretty strange yourself,' she said, squeezing my arm as we walked along.

'No, just pretty cold,' I said. 'Wish I'd put on more clothes.'

'I gather you've lost your boxer shorts already.'

'Who told you that? You haven't got private investigators out, have you?'

'Sarah told me. She says you've blamed everyone in the family.'

'Oh no, she didn't grab you as well, did she?'

These shorts were a present from Isabella, rather forward, I thought, but very smart, my only garment of passing fashion, passing passion.

'She told me at school. I think she's very interesting.

Obviously very clever. That's where the brains in the family have gone.'

'Ha ha,' I said. 'Anyway, they'll turn up. Probably stuck in that stupid washing-machine.'

'You seem to lose a lot of things.'

'Look, are you trying to get at me? I don't have to walk with you, you know. I'm just doing it to keep warm. Come on, give me a cuddle.'

I did get a quick hug, but that was all. It made me feel a bit warmer for a few moments.

'Huh, call this Easter?' I said. 'I put on my best Benetton button-down shirt, just to impress you. Wish I'd put on me Dad's thermals.'

'Well, walk properly, push back your shoulders, don't slouch, then you might feel a bit warmer.'

'Oh God, not more criticism.'

'So now he's paranoid as well.'

'No, just freezing. Come on, I'll treat you to a Guinness.'

We'd come to the Palace Pier and I could see the bar was open. It's my new affectation, drinking Guinness. One day I might even like it.

'Let's not go inside. Let's keep in the fresh air, not huddle in a smoky bar.'

'Fresh air, you're joking. This wind could make the North Pole feel as stale as the inside of the Northern Line.'

I'm glad she doesn't smoke, what a comfort. I hate all smokers and can smell their nasty clothes a mile away. Her drinking problem is a worry, though. That is, she doesn't. She only drinks when she really feels like it, funny gel. I've been brought up, thanks to Lol and other eager teachers back in the fifth year, to drink whether I like it or not, whether I want it or not, just like other appetites we need not go into. It's what being a MAN is all about, innit.

So we walked and walked, hand in hand; now and again my hand strayed into her pocket, as I'd also forgotten my gloves, not my fault, and the feel of her moving, walking, breathing body, even through fifteen layers, made me tremulous, but I said no, it's just the shivers, I think I could have caught flu.

We came to this little door in the wall, under the promenade bit, beside the deck-chairs and saucy postcards and candy-floss. There was a brightly painted notice-board outside, announcing the presence of the one and only, friend of the stars, Madame Isabella.

'So that's what you do after school,' I said. 'Better than knackering your hands with an ice-cream scooop.'

I laughed, ha ha ha, in my brittle, cynical fashion, mocking all the words and the quotes from the stars, then walked on: how silly, how soppy, how can anyone take any of that sort of nonsense seriously?

'Hold on,' she said.

She stood there, getting out her purse, examining her change. She'd come out with more than me, not hard to do as I had only a quid left and was banking on her for a sub, should there be any emergencies, such as special-offer Guinness.

'You're not going in, bloody hell. I thought you were intelligent, I thought you had sense, you must be off your rocker.'

It cost her £10. I knew you'd be shocked. I could hardly speak for fury. Still, it's her life, her future, her money. She was out in fifteen minutes, which made me more furious. Think what I could have done with ten quidlets.

'Any good? What load of old cobblers did she tell you?'

'Actually, she wasn't very good. I've had better.'

'You mean to say that wasn't your first time? You've been stupid enough to get done before? You must be potty.'

'If you're going to be like that, I'm not going to discuss it with you. Don't criticize things you don't understand.'

'Come on then, explain it to me, make me understand, in words of few syllables.'

'You've got no sensitivity. You just rubbish everything straight away.'

'O K then, I promise not to laugh or giggle or mock or make any comment. Just tell me. Anything. Oh, come on.'

'Unlike you,' she began slowly, taking my hand out of her pocket, walking alone, pulling her coat around her, 'I do believe in the existence of extra-sensory perception, that there is a sort of field out there, through which some people can communicate in a way that other people still can't understand or explain.'

I held back; wait a bit, Cartner, don't blunder in, this could be serious, she *is* off her rocker.

'That time in the caff when you served me, there was a communication between us that day.'

I'd felt the same, of course I had, but I don't tell people such soppy things, only to Uncle WP. But I managed to keep quiet, arrange my serious face, my concerned, nay, sensitive look. Never knew I had one.

'I know you're mocking. I don't need to look at you. But that's it. We won't discuss it again.'

She increased her step and walked off ahead of me. I ran after her, but she wouldn't talk or look at me or accept my hand, pushing me away. I'd noticed these sudden changes of mood before, but this was silly. It hadn't even been a proper discussion, no real arguments over real subjects, not like some we've had in the last two weeks. All so very silly and trivial. I don't actually give a toss about palm-reading.

I walked on my own for a while, tramping and trudging, moving towards a touch of the moodies, which would be fatal. If we both did that, the whole day would be finished. I passed several beach photographers who tried to interest me in having my photograph taken, but I refused, though I knew Isabella would have liked it. They all looked pretty scruffy. One of them in the distance seemed to be an old woman, but I couldn't see if she had a monkey or not. I might have stopped for that.

I did stop at a beach shelter, on the side of which some-one had written a message in huge letters: 'I FEEL A BIT NORMAL TODAY'. I hid behind it, waiting for Isabella to catch up with me, then I jumped out at her, pretending to be an old biddy.

'Oooh, you've got a lucky face, missus,' I said, in my best old woman's voice, putting my scarf up and over my head so she could hardly see my face. I ran right in front of her and grabbed her hand.

'Oooh, now what I can see in this lovely palm? Hold on dear, don't be shy, I have got extra-terrestrial receptions. Seating upstairs, at all prices. No, don't resist. Your lifeline is very good, yes I think you are going to have a life, one of those ones which begins with birth and goes on till, let me see, closing-time. Before that happens a tall dark stranger is going to come along, be very dominant and whisk you away dear, then you'll end up happy ever after . . .'

She burst out laughing and gave me a slap on the face, but ever so gentle, ever so affectionate.

'I didn't want to tell you, as you'll just crow. But she *did* say that – two tall, dark strangers will come into my life and be very dominant.'

'Why didn't you pay me? I'd have told you all that for a fiver, and given tokens.'

'I knew you'd just mock.'

'No, no, come on, I promise to listen properly.'

'The only thing that was interesting was that she didn't say whether the tall, dark strangers were men or women. No sex was mentioned.'

'I should hope not.'

'She made it clear she couldn't tell, just these strong, domi-nant figures. So that was different.'

'This is the modern age, ducky. This is Brighton.'

And so to the station, to catch the last possible train back to

London, what a nice day, some good chats, some good times, a hell of a lot of good walks, all of them ending up hand in hand, tra-la, but it did mean I was absolutely ravenous. How had I lasted so long.

'I'll see you on the train,' I shouted, as she went through the barrier. 'You go ahead and bag a good seat, non-smoking.'

She thought I was going to the lav again, on the hour all day, no wonder in that freezing cold, but I headed for the hamburger counter on the left, nasty smell, dodgy-looking stuff, but needs must, a man has to have sustenance, a stomach cannot survive on romantic chat alone.

'You are not sitting beside me, eating that,' she said.

I'd blown the last of my money, a whole pound, gone pleasure-mad. I thought at first she was joking, affectionate fun, so I just smirked, opened the burger, let her see all the gunge inside, opened my gob, let her see where it was all going.

'That's it,' she said.

She got up, left the carriage and went off on her own. And I didn't see her again till Victoria.

Oh, God, here we go again, am I up to all this, all this heavy stuff? I'm only little, I just want to be quietly happy, not endure all this up-and-down, roller-coaster emotional stuff.

As we approached Victoria I stiffened the sinews, banished my false pride, softened the old blood and went off down the train to find her.

'I'm very sorry. It was inconsiderate. I should not have done it.'

Hey ho, didn't mean a word of it, but that's what life and loving is like. She didn't look at me, or admit my presence, staring hard out of the dark, dirty window, knowing I didn't mean a word of it.

'No, honestly. I do regret it. I wish I hadn't had any of it.

I feel sick. I wasn't really hungry anyway. It was greed. Something to do, just 'cos I saw it.'

All true this time. And she knew it. She slowly got up, smiled rather wearily, and together we walked, hand in hand, to the tube.

Just as well we were friends again. Just as well the row was over. As we queued up for tickets, still hand in hand, we discovered neither of us had any money left. She'd blown all hers on that stupid I mean, perspicacious – Madame Isabella. I'd wasted mine on the sodium glutamate.

We walked home. Took us almost two hours. As if we hadn't done enough walking that day. I was totally knackered by the time we got to her house, with her helping me the last half-mile of the way.

When this romance finishes (what am I saying? Please, God, it never will) I'll be ready for the Olympics, marathon road-walk division. And other assorted mental and emotional tests. Love is a many splendoured thing, but gee, it can be tiring. In so many ways. EXIT, shattered.

8 An Awful Happening

'You're very iffy tonight,' said my mum.

'Even iffier than usual,' said my dad.

'You're a right pain in the arse, if you ask me,' said Sarah.

'Language,' said my mum.

'Sod off, the lot of you,' I said.

'More language,' said my dad. Another day, another wonderful family meal.

Not sure about the derivation of 'iffy'. We in our little nuclear family use it when someone is being mildly bad-tempered, irritable, not their usual sunny selves. It can also refer to the weather when it doesn't know what it's going to do. So that's about it; now into Round Two.

My dad was stuffing his stupid face. You'd have thought at his age he would be beyond such things, that greed would have left him, the battles for seconds in life all over. I s'pose it's what keeps him going. Something must. Can't see much point otherwise.

Sez is a veggie, has been for well over an hour, all the fashion in her fifth year. So is the O W, but not for any deep philosophical or intellectual or religious reasons. Purely aesthetic. She has decided that all meat looks unattractive, steak most of all. Now, vegetables and fruit, awfully pretty-looking, don't you think? And frightfully good for you.

Moi, I'm off meat at the moment. I haven't felt hungry at all these last few days, in fact I'm off quite a few things. I still like chicken and all fish, are you in the picture? That leaves the O F, our Big Guzzler. He has all the meat to himself, when there is any. He always wolfs it down like a pig, in a panic, then the next panic is to make sure he gets his fair share of the vegetables, which have been made and lovingly prepared for our pure veggie friends, not for him.

As for the wine, that is unbelievable. He marks the wine bottle with a ruler and pen, so that the O W does not have more than her fair share. He practically cries if he thinks he's been cheated out of half a centimetre. She, of course, maintains that she does not drink, that she's given it up, but she's as bad as he is, fiddling the marks, drinking behind his back. Personally, I think they're both alcoholics.

Yet they complain about me, now and again, coming home after having a few. Yes, I was once sick on the upstairs landing and yes, she had to clean it up, but no one asked her, I would have done it in the morning, or the afternoon, or the next day. It was my first sixth-form social, lower sixth. I'm never allowed to forget it.

I also hate his jaw. Yes, I know he can't help it. He has to take it with him. It's the noise, the clicking, the way he masticates like a demented cow, chewing at triple speed as if the end of the world is coming and he's heard there's rationing in Heaven.

My mother's irritating habits, now, let me think, you

don't want to hear, I know, you want to hear about other things; hard Cheddar, you'll have to wait. Just like me. Her faults are more verbal. She never lets up. You can programme her to say almost anything; pick one from twenty topics, select twenty possible reactions, then permute and off she goes, and up comes the answer that you know from the first that she'll come up with, but she trots it out, all glowing and virtuous as if she has reached a penetrating and original response.

If I say I feel full, her response is, you should not have had that cake before your supper. I think I've got flu: you should have put your coat on last night, as I told you. I feel sick: you should not have had all that cheese. I've got no money: you should not have spent it at the pub. I feel tired: stay out till two in the morning, no wonder you're tired.

She's actually quite good at helping, at suggesting things, but first you have to listen to her stating the obvious, going back over the ancient past, telling you what you did wrong when you already know, instead of taking it forward. If you complain about this and say, look, give us a break, she replies, you brought the subject up, Cartner, you asked my opinion. No I didn't, Mother, I was simply clearing my brain, putting you in the picture. If I'd wanted a commentary, I would have hired David Coleman. Oh God, is there no more pudding? What a house.

Then I bang out. There's often a race to bang out, as Sez is now at that certain age. The OF has threatened to take the hinges off the living-room door if it goes on any longer.

'No, I'm not playing snooker with you tonight,' I shouted. 'And don't shout. You know I've got a headache. I'm too tired. Anyway, you're useless.'

They love family meals, goodness knows why. I suppose we do get away with most things, as long as we turn up vaguely on time and are vaguely polite to them. When I'm a father, I'll allow anyone who wants to to sit with their food in front of the telly. I think it's only respectful to the produ-cers and directors. All that work they've put into the pro-grammes, yet some people sit with their backs to the screen, talking amongst themselves, letting it blare away. Not in our house, of course. It's off during all meals. Ditto the phone. Potty, isn't it? She actually unplugs the phone while we eat. Sez goes absolutely spare.

Sez's solution, her way of getting through these happy family meals, is to hum. Strange, really. I don't think she even knows she hums. Just a tuneless tune, over and over again. I get bad-tempered and more yobbish: why, I have even been known to be downright iffy. Especially at the moment. At least Sez has suddenly become kinder to me, almost civilized, not sure why.

My mood has nothing whatsoever to do with my dad's disgusting eating habits, nor my mother's self-righteousness. We have had that at meal-times for decades. I happen to be utterly dejected and fed up and worried about something completely else. Not that they know. Not that I'd tell anyone. Isabella has disappeared.

So hello, WP, how you doin tonight, long time no screen-time. Well, I haven't had a lot to tell you.

I should now, of course, be getting that essay done, put-ting in some revision. It's just that for these last five days, when I've failed to find her, I've been unable to do any-thing.

And how are you, room? You had some good times during those two magical weeks, with your cheerful little occupant, coming home to see you every night. Give me some of it back now, when I need it.

I've been ringing her constantly, since she didn't turn up at school on Monday. A cold, I thought, or flu. How ironic. It was me who complained all the time about the Brighton breezes.

I rang on Monday first, late in the evening, and got her mum, who is foreign. I could hear various people jabbering on in the background, but I got no sense out of her. I didn't find it too worrying. That's how she is on the phone.

Next day, still no sign of Isabella, so I rang again straight after school, and this time I was told by a voice that she wasn't there. Ah, so she couldn't be ill, that's something. If she's out, wherever, that must be a good sign. Or is it?

She doesn't take all the same subjects as me, only English. Many teachers now let you stay at home and give you revision work, what with the exams being so close. Perhaps she's gone somewhere quiet.

Next day I went round to the library, thinking she might be working there, getting a bit of peace, as she's always complaining she can't work at home for all her relations. No sign of her. No one had seen her for weeks, and I asked everyone, even the tramps.

At school I asked Clarissa, but she knew nothing. I rang some of the people in Isabella's French and Art classes, which was hard, as people are not turning up all the time, but they knew nothing either.

So, another evening's sitting here, moping, pretending to work, pretending to tell you things, but what is there to tell you, old WP?

Oh no. A terrible but very obvious thought has just struck me. It's the bum's rush. Goodbye, Cartner, it was nice knowing you. Or not knowing you.

I didn't really know her. I don't really know her, not in the sense I think you mean. I refuse to go into that, anyway. Some things are sacred. Some things are scared. And some things are scarred. Any more letters I can press?

No, she wouldn't do that. She would have let me know, a girl of such principles and moral behaviour. I do know that much.

I find it hard and rather humiliating now to have to admit

that her 'going out' with Lol meant nothing. I'd got it all wrong in my stupid head.

She's recently taken up the saxophone, moving on from the clarinet, in which she passed grade five and was triffic, but she grew to hate all the practising and heavy stuff she had to play. So she decided to start on the saxophone, from scratch. Lol ever so kindly suggested she could sit in with the school jazz band, where he is the leader, so he says, the star drummer. She soon found out how useless they all were, especially Lol. So she got a teacher, a proper saxophone player, that black bloke I saw her with in the flats. All perfectly innocent. Wish I could play an instrument. Play anything. Play, not mope.

Ring, ring.

I jumped up, rushed out of my room to the landing and crashed into Sez, who was also rushing for the phone.

'You're very keen on the phone all of a sudden,' she said. 'What's bugging you, who are you expecting, huh? Has that boring Annabella gone off with someone else? Ha ha ha.'

Back to normal, and I thought she was being nice to me for once. And who told her anyway? That Lol, probably.

I gave her a shove, not very hard or very serious, but she fell over one of her own stupid ornaments and made a hell of a noise, hammed it all up. The Wrinklies rushed out of the woodwork and wanted to know what all the commotion was about, all this horseplay, how old were we, anyway?

I grabbed the phone at last, though I could hardly hear for Sez crashing around in her room and the Wrinklies shouting up the stairs. It was a wrong number.

What am I going to do tomorrow night, Saturday night, when it won't be all right, without my love-heart. But was she? Have I imagined it all? What about those rows and arguments, storming off, annoying each other. We have different tastes, different habits. Our footsteps are not even in time.

That was a surprise, though why should any two human

beings, meeting at random, have the same walk. All along the Brighton front I tried to click into gear, get in step with her, but my steps are quicker, poncier, jerkier, always ahead of her slower, measured, longer, more sedate paces. It would have been neat, so I told her, to match our walks, a sign, a symbol, a good portent. I thought you did not believe in such things, she replied quickly. Got me there, WP, didn't she just, yup, that sussed me.

More worrying, more disappointing, is the fact that our hearts are not in tune either. I mean mechanically, pound pound pound, beat beat beat. I discovered we have different rhythms. As we lay together one night – please, please, do not jump to any conclusions, I'm trying to be serious, even sensitive for once – I listened for a long time, as our hearts both thudded. Yours would have thudded as well. Anybody's would have done. On her mum's couch, with ten thousand strange relations in the next room, just waiting for some pretext so they could barge in.

The family is Catholic. Not sure what I am. Nothing, I think. I could be Wee Free or Seventh Day Adventist. I must look up my vaccination card some time. (We don't talk about such things in our house. We've got more important things to argue about at meal-times, such as the wine.) But that is not a problem between us. Isabella doesn't mind. She's told me she's agnostic. I've said I support Spurs. But it does mean that her family keep a rather close eye on her, and she does try to respect their wishes and traditions.

Could that be it? Is that what's come between us? Your actual Romeo and Juliet, the Capulets and the whatever they were called. Long time since I've seen *West Side Story*. Hated the book. Loved the musical.

I've just rung again, no reply, they must have hung up, fed up with me calling. Ah well, better do some work, put in some time, shove an essay together, copy out of two books instead of the usual one. It's called research.

Oh, bloody hell. I'm going to scream and shout and throw things. I hate you, ceiling. Get lost, room. You're a fraud, WP, nothing but a nasty, heartless, vacuous, uncaring bloody machine. Why did I trust you and tell you anything? What has happened? This was supposed to be the start. What's gone wrong? Why the hell is she avoiding me?

9 Musings and McDonalds

I'm going out for a bit and I may not be back for a long time. I'm heading down those mean streets, round these ugly blocks, along our scruffy pavements, amongst your litter, passing all our human rubbish. So attractive just a week ago. Walking home from Victoria, however knackered, it had seemed almost exciting, heart of the universe, this throbbing metropolis. Now I'm emigrating. No point in staying here. I need to get away. TO FIND MYSELF. Where's me bike?

I decided just to look round myself for a bit, admire the exterior, inspect the scaffolding, the pipes and the heating, then perhaps a quick poke around the central nervous system, looking out for any faults in the heart of the building. Was it my fault? Is it all delusions?

If only I had a job, I could fill in the whole afternoon, put in the day, use up the night, occupy all the gaps in my brain. Saturday; it's going to be this sort of Saturday for ever, probably.

I had small French fries in McDonalds, eking out my money, sitting hard against the wall in the corner, back to the world. Oh, isn't that Cartner Livingstone, upper-sixth pseud, all on his own? Can't be, sitting in that sort of place, Saturday night, he must be desperate. He hasn't cracked up has he, he's not on crack is he? Must be those exams, pathetic creature, don't look at him children, it's not a pretty sight.

Nobody did see, nobody spoke, so I just sat and listened. Two old biddies at the table behind me, both in blue raincoats, probably only forty-four, but they looked sixty-four, smoking like mad, talking through their fags to each other, only stopping to belt and chastise two little kids, their grandchildren probably, in cheap, white fur coats, who were stuffing themselves with milk shakes.

'I've only got eggs in the house,' said one of them. 'But I tell you what, I'll make them with salad cream, the way you like it.'

I could smell the hamburgers and the smoke long afterwards. Hey ho, I suppose I could be in Ethiopia, or have only one leg in the house. Not that again. Sometimes I sound like my mum. I hate counting blessings. Bugger blessings.

I stared through shop windows, observing Indian families, the women hovering in saris in the background, looking worried and confused, the young lads cocky and sharp but caught like flies in the family net. The windows are barred, the displays dusty and faded, but the shop door is always open, waiting for a sale, ready in case some late-night reveller runs out of John Player Specials or is desperate for another dirty video. How can Life possibly be better here?

Perhaps I'm gay.

Now how did that enter my head. What sparked off that thought. I play this game with Isabella (remember her? I

hardly can) in which we trace back each little, sudden, uncon-
nected thought, tracking down the sliver that slipped into
the brain by a side door and set up a whole new train of
nonsense and *non sequiturs*. *My Beautiful Launderette*.
That must be it. I saw it with Her, my Beloved, my former
Once and Future, but that's not the connection. It was
simply staring and wondering at those sad, soulful Indian
boys.

It could explain a lot. Such as why I didn't give Tracey
one. Or two, fitting in Karen for afters, or even durings.
Real men eat women. And what about Marie, why was I so
appalled. Lol would not have bothered, no time for thank
you, Ma'am, just wham, bam, now try this for size. Sensitivity or repression?

The whole teenage world is at it, so there must be some
reason why I'm not. You just have to read the figures that
they churn out all the time when they're hard up for news.
Let's have a teenage survey, and don't forget to ask about
their sex life, oh, and get a few pop stars to comment, they'll
tell you anything you want, and afterwards they won't deny
anything they never said.

It is a truth universally acknowledged that all happy teenagers are happy in the same way, but all unhappy teenagers
are different. Would make a good context question. Or has
it been used already? I should really do an essay plan first,
that's what Barnes says. It's supposed to be best to work in
some facts at the beginning of every essay, that's if you can't
begin with a quotation. So let's go: over 93 percent of young
people interviewed ceased to be virgins at the age of thirteen
and three quarters: 35 percent lost their virginity to a fifteen-
year-old baby-sitter, 26 percent did it first behind the bike
sheds, while the remaining 22 percent could not remember,
but will probably be voting SDP at the next election.

Being gay, hmm, could explain a lot.

There was that time on the school camp, the rotten one

in Wales when it poured down all the time. I'd gone out with Silas, of all people, late at night; we sneaked into the village when we were not supposed to, then sneaked back again because everything was closed. We got lost, the rain was terrible, the lane was pitch-black and we got scared, so we sang songs to cheer ourselves up. Then we held hands. All the way home. It was just something that suddenly happened. For comfort, friendship, or out of fear? I've never told anyone, nor has Silas. Not even Isabella. Now why not, if she's my friend? Was my friend. Rather suspicious.

Worse happened during that hol, or what can be made to sound worse, such as Lol trying to assault me on the bunk-bed after he'd strolled around naked, showing his bum, pretending to be a woman, when the rest of us barely knew what a woman was. That was just your knock-about, third-form vulgarity. Lol is as normal as . . . but let me think: is he, could he be, is all his boasting a cover? There again, who cares? But for some reason that far more innocent, harmless, minor act of holding hands has stuck in my mind. I liked it.

On the other hand, I have become besotted, dreaming about her, scheming about her. I'd be fancying some feller, wouldn't I, or does it not happen that way? I don't know. I haven't seen enough films. I could be both. I don't know what I am or where I'm going.

I wish someone had left chalk marks on the ground in front of me, a few signposts. Come in, Madame Isabella, you are needed at last, I'm a Believer, oh yes I am, I'm a Believer. Now who sang that?

I did a few steps round a lamppost and stepped over a few dossers, just missing a few bottles, a few bundles, a few dead bodies. Am I still wandering around Camden Town? Could have sworn I was in the Waste Land with Uncle Tom Eliot and all. Another load of old nonsense. How do they get away with it.

A tall, dark stranger. Has he come along and whisked her away? That boring Madame Rotguts could be right. Curse her, cursor. Hey, that's my first WP joke. I can't be as depressed as I'm telling myself, so he told himself.

Oh, if only this WP had a Fast Forward button. It will, oh yes it will. One day I'll be able to zoom ahead, to see what I'm going to write and going to live before it happens. Would I press it? Would I want to know? At this moment I would. This moment is hell, so what have I got to lose by peeping at the next moment? I'd like to know if I should write END, here and now, that's it, friends and enemies and strangers, no more story, no more anything. EXIT, FINISH EDIT AND PRINT.

I'll have a look at the master MENU: perhaps an unseen hand has CREATED NEW DOCUMENT while I've been wandering around, filled in the future for me, revealed where she has gone, why she has left me. Nope, nothing that I can find, unless it's in there crouching in one of the HIDDEN FILES, in that blessed state of LIMBO that the handbook talks about. Haven't worked that out yet. Never will. Life is too short to read a 624-page PCW 9512 Personal Computer Word Processor User Guide.

I've come to a serious conclusion, Mr Amstrad. I hate to say it, as we've never met, and I know you're very successful and have sold lots of your wonderful machines and folks swear by you and cross their hearts and say you've changed their lives, but I honestly think – no, don't interrupt. You are a PLONKER. And so is everyone else who uses a WP. Over and out.

I found myself outside her house. You know what it's like, lost in thought, lost in reveries, the foot leads the brain, the wish becomes the fulfilment. Not quite a house. A three-room flat. Hard to categorize it. I know it's rented, 'cos she told me, but it's a private little block, modern, boring, but fairly desirable I suppose, if you like living in a concrete rabbit hutch. The Russians do. It's the sort of anonymous place they have up in Highgate. In fact, I think she told me that there's a Russian on the floor below.

Could she be a member of the KGB? She's been sent to spy on me, get the secrets of my A-level revision course and has now passed them to the Russkies. Or has she by mistake got mixed up in a more complicated little plot, or seen something she should not have?

She could, of course, be part of one of *our* little plots. I wouldn't put anything past MI6. Now they're part of show business, they think they can do anything. You read about them all the time. Dead letter-boxes, hidden films, innocent people pricked in the bum with loaded umbrellas. Are her relations in on it, or in on something? I never got them straight. The plot sickens.

I looked up at her window, first floor, no lights on. All the ground-floor windows have grilles, plus burglar alarms, plus Neighbourhood Watch stickers. Probably trip-wires on every plate, alarms on every teaspoon. What a world we live in.

'Er, it's me, Cartner, just passing and I wondered if Isabella was in . . .'

I must have pressed the wrong flat number. It was very dark and I could hardly make out the numbers and names on the little entryphone thing. A deep guttural voice said, 'Ya'.

I repeated my query, in case her mother had acquired a deep guttural voice since last I spoke to her.

'Go away,' said the Ya voice, 'or I will call the police.'

I saw a light go on on the second floor, could hear doors opening and people talking, so I decided to do a quick walk round the block. I'm too young and precious for an umbrella up the bum.

I returned about ten minutes later and made sure I pressed

the right button this time, Flat Three. I could hear the entry-phone being picked up and someone listening to me as I blurted out my inquiry, then it was hung up again. Silence.

I was still bending down, listening to the silence, when a large man approached from behind. What a fright. I hadn't heard him come up the steps. I jumped about a mile in the air.

No, I wasn't hit on the head, nor drugged and taken off to South America, nor did he flash his card and say I'm a double double double agent working for the notorious Miss Button, keep quiet if you know what's good for you. He simply walked straight past me, opened the door with his key and went in and up the stairs. He never even glanced at me.

I moved away, down the short flight of steps; that's it, might as well give up.

The front door was still creaking electronically on its hinges, closing ever so slowly, then coming to a temporary halt with a one-inch gap still showing. Enough for my little fingers? Back I went, up the steps, and pushed open the front door.

I'll hear her crying, I thought, that'll be it, behind a locked door, or she'll call out when she realizes it's me. I am being held a captive here, help, oh help, brave Lord Cartner, prithee stay, I'll let down my long golden hair betwixt the burglar alarms, be careful of those dreaded iron bars, pray do not spike your precious loins, then you can climb up and rescue me, oh, my hero, you have come at last, I always knew you would.

I banged softly on the front door of her flat, trying to work out explanations in my head: how the front door had been left wide open, or should I say another resident had insisted I come in?

I banged again, this time not as softly, but it still did not open. I realized I was being watched through a spyhole by someone or something. They could see me and, presumably, didn't like what they could see.

'Go away,' said the voice. I bleated out my question once again.

'Eesabell does not want to see you. She say no to come, she no want you to visit no more.'

'What?' I said, trying to be as slow and stupid as possible. 'Is she okay, is she ill? What's happened to her? I just want to know.'

'Just go away. She no want you.'

Well, that was it. Sod her. Why should I care. Why should I hang around and depress myself. Forget it, once and for all. I'm just being pathetic, not taking the hint, nay, the command. She's made it pretty clear. But what a way to finish. Never thought it would be like that, not from her, not for me.

So I'm home. Where else is there to go. Straight home. And then I wrote a letter to her. I have a copy somewhere, now in limbo. No one else will want to see it, all part of the sordid past.

I even put it through her letter-box, some two hours ago. I've now tied everything up, finished the parcel, sealed the knots. In the letter I told her I was chucking her. Yes, child-ish, silly, don't say it. But come on, think of the way she's treated me. I wanted the satisfaction of me ending it, or telling myself I was ending it. Why ever did I get mixed up with that sort. Cheers, WP. I won't be talking to you again, not for a long time. What else is there to tell you? Nada, rien.

Oh no, there's the phone, just as I was dropping off. Not even Sez is answering it. She's silent in her room for once. Wrong number I bet.

'It's me,' said the voice. *Peep-peep-peep.*

What? What's happening? On a pay phone? I thought she

was at home. I could hear clunks and clicks as she struggled to get more money in. Where can she be?

'It's me,' she said again, with more noise and clicks in the background. 'I got your letter. I'm sorry.'

Long silence.

'So am I sorry,' I said. 'Sorry about everything.'

'I can't tell you, not yet, that's why you're right, in your letter, it's the best way, the only way, so we'd better finish. You won't want to see me ever again.'

'Course I do, don't be daft. I've got to. Just once. I've got to know. You might as well tell me to my face.'

'I can't.'

'Where are you?'

More *peep-peeps* and noises. The conversation had not made sense anyway. What the hell was she playing at? Where could she be.

But this time she was cut off completely. All I could make out was one word.

Zunz.

10 A Visit to the Hospital

I went up in the lift, or tried to. There was a row of them, but each took for ever to arrive and when one did there was a mad scramble, and I lost out twice. Not like me, not to push and shove. Perhaps I wasn't in a hurry to find out whatever it was I was going to find out.

I decided to walk up, which was silly, as they'd hidden the stairs, and no wonder. In the public bits it's like the Hilton Hotel, all plush and warm, if a bit battered and in need of painting. The stairs are brutal and concrete and cold, the truth behind the exterior, the reality you don't usually see. Like Isabella? Was I now about to meet the real her, in person, at last?

Could *she* be gay? That would explain it. All night I'd examined everything we'd done together, sniffed around the signs and worried over the pointers. After all, I don't know her. As you know (because I've told you, and you believe everything I tell you), none of that carnal stuff had taken place, not for want of thinking, or even trying. But I'm still not going to go into that. Anyway, it just sort of didn't happen.

I know from Lol, and ten million other Lols, that these days it all begins with It. You start with bed, then slowly, if you're still speaking, you speak, find out about each other. With us, we've taken each game as it comes, Brian, got inside the penalty box, hit the bar a few times, but neither of us has been in a blind rush to score. Too precious for that. So I thought. But I could be wrong, about me, or about her, about the things she said, things she said no to, things she told me not to do.

I've been here once before, but only once, to visit my mum. She was having something done to her, down there, women's stuff, which me and Sarah were not supposed to be told about, thank goodness. Who wants to be told about that? They can keep it a secret for ever, as far as I'm concerned. Hmm. Is that another indication of my true nature, abhorring the wonderful mystery of womanhood, or am I just chickening out? I was only eleven. But Mum was in Zunz. That's how I knew. The very same ward. How weird. How not very wonderful.

I've always remembered the name Zunz because it doesn't look like a name, more like a number, East Ukrainian for Zero. Spurs five, Sporting Kroks zunz. I expect the ward is named after some old biddy called Mrs Zunz. All the wards in the Royal Free Hospital are like that. I suppose they are in most places. I think I'd rather have a hotel bedroom named after me, or a brothel, not a boring old hospital ward. The Cartner Livingstone Memorial Bonking Room.

What a lot of nice, empty little rooms there are here. Never realized that. Look at them, changing rooms, disabled lavs, showers with good locks, ample wash-rooms, so many secret places where you could shut yourself in and no one would ever know what you were doing.

I was lost again. Wondering about the possibilities, I'd wandered out on to the wrong floor. Hospitals are so easy to walk round. No one ever checks, no one ever asks who you are or what your business is, squire. Me and Is could have come here instead of freezing ourselves on Brighton front, hanging round the streets, standing against trees on the Heath. Even a hospital shower must be better than her living-room couch. If we'd discovered this all those weeks ago, we might not have remained – now choose the word carefully, I don't want any sniggering, Lol, take the grin off your ugly mush – VIRGINS. There, I said it. Why dissemble.

I got to the seventh floor at last, but I couldn't find her bed. I wandered in upon an old man having a bed bath, and got out sharpish. Wards are all mixed these days. Then an old woman called me from a little ward of four beds to help with her dress, and I went over, ready to do what I could till I realized she was potty, completely wandering. But aren't we all, love.

Then I saw her, sitting half-turned away from me, reading beside her bed, in a little foursome ward. Two old women were asleep, comatose, all strapped up, if not dead. The other bed was empty.

As she turned, I could see that her whole face had been horrifically damaged and her neck and head and shoulders were swathed in bandages. She looked away for a moment, quickly, caught off her guard, not expecting me, not on a Sunday morning, anyway, before the normal visiting hours. Then she looked towards me, smiled bravely, sadly, then shook her head and pursed her lips as if to say, go away, don't look, don't come any nearer.

'What does the other girl look like?' I found myself saying.

What a stupid remark, how cretinous. I just wanted to be jocular, not heavy and all Hospital Visitorish, make her smile, make her know it's me, her old mate, her soul mate, so I thought, so I hoped.

I went slowly over towards her, stopped, grinned feebly and looked around inanely. I found a chair in a corner and dragged it across so I could sit beside her, trying hard to take my eyes off her injuries, to pretend I hadn't even noticed them.

'Not a bad little ward. Any sign of Michael Foot? I thought he had a season ticket to the Free. What's the food like. Is Room Service any better these days, hmm . . .'

She looked at me, sighed, put down her book and slowly stood up, leaning against the bed for support.

She pulled her NHS-issue dressing-gown around her, covering as much of her arms and neck as possible, and led me out of the ward, down the corridor and into a little day-room. The smell of smoke hung from every wall like funeral drapes. The atmosphere of the empty room was filled with ill people, long since decayed and departed.

I looked around to check there was no one else in the room, no biddies slumped in a corner, but there was just the TV blaring away, some stupid Sunday morning children's show, *Pob's Programme*. We tried to put it off but failed, so we retreated to a corner to be on our own, to be together, to wait and see.

As we talked, I kept on half seeing, half listening to the television. Quite a good little story, actually, about a tortoise that refuses to hibernate. How could you, Cartner, at a time like that? But I did. I was half watching it. I think she was too tired, too resigned to realize or protest.

'I told my mother,' she said, 'to say I didn't want to see you again.'

'I know, she told me. In the end. Taken me all week to find out. I was so worried. What happened?'

'I don't want to see you. It's true. I'd like you to go now.'

'Don't be daft,' I said, trying an encouraging, friendly, concerned smile. 'Anyway, I want to know what happens to that stupid tortoise.'

There was no smile, no reaction. I don't think she even understood my silly remark.

'So what did happen?' I asked.

'Nothing.'

'Ho hum, now you're being silly.'

'I got mugged.'

I looked at her, then looked around, not listening to the television any more, not feeling the smoke or sensing the dead bodies.

'In those flats?' I asked. 'Your saxophone lesson?'

The scene had already flashed into my mind. Looking back, it had always been there, a lurking image, an ominous warning, right from that moment I'd seen her on the landing.

'Well, you're alive and well,' I said at last. 'As well as can be expected. Best hospital in Europe. They'll soon have you up and out and playing for the first team. They were brilliant with my mother. She loved it here. Now, which was her bed? She didn't want to come home. She had such a good time. She still sees two of the women who were in with her. They have reunions . . .'

I was gabbling on, relieved really. It was now perfectly clear what had happened, terrible and awful, but at least now I could see how her mind had been running.

She thought I wouldn't want to see her with her face all bashed up, that I would be appalled by the sight of her injuries. Rather hurtful, believing I'd react like that, but, of course, she must also be in shock, poor thing. We'll both emigrate. This country has had it.

'After the exams,' I said, 'let's go round Europe, just the two of us, for three months. I saved all my Saturday money. I was going to buy new trainers, but what the hell, this is more important. I can lend you some if you want. And I've got some Savings Certs my gran left me. I fancy Turkey, supposed to be really good, what do you think, hmm?'

'I think I'd better get back to bed. Sister said I hadn't to walk much or get exhausted.'

She got up and made for the door. The television tortoise was now in someone's kitchen, sliding around on the polished floor. It looked very funny.

'Well, I've told you now,' she said, sighing heavily, clutching her stomach, feeling her bandages. She was back in her little ward, getting into bed.

'So you should,' I said. 'You should have told me it all at the beginning, when it happened.'

She looked at me for a long time, thinking. I wasn't sure if she was going to doze off, or if her injuries were so painful that her eyes were glazed from pain.

'I haven't told you all of it.'

'Come on, then. I'm a big boy.

'I'd like you to go. And not come back again. I mean it.'

'Look, don't be potty. I'm sorry I was half looking at that stupid programme. Just nerves, really. I hate hospitals. Anyway, what do you mean, "not all of it" . . .?'

'I told you. Go now, please.'

'Well, if you insist. I might just catch the end of the tortoise . . .'

She burst out crying. Oh, God. I had been dreading that from the moment I arrived, prattling on to prevent any tears from starting.

She then told me the rest of the story: enough, more than enough, about what happened to her that night she was attacked in the lift by two blokes.

Then I burst into tears. Didn't help, did it? No one wants some visitor blubbering all over the ward. Sister certainly did not.

She sent me home. She explained that Isabella was in such a distressed state that it would be best if I didn't come again, till Sister thought it would be all right. Such as another week, Saturday perhaps. Then it might be all right.

*

I've been lying on my bed, looking at the ceiling, wondering if I should tell you all this. I've been seeing pictures I have not seen since I was seven, like that horrible face in the corner where the cornice is broken. The pictures scared me at one time, and I had to suck my cloth for comfort.

I have it somewhere, just a piece of rag, really, as far as Sarah was concerned. What a pig she was when I used to cry for it, mocking me for being a baby. It came from a Spurs towel, which I got for Christmas when I was six. I used it so much it was soon in shreds, but I kept one bit of it to cuddle, to get me to sleep. In the morning it was always sodden where I'd been sucking it.

I'll find it now. Haven't used it recently, but I've got it hidden in my underpants drawer, in case Sez ever finds out I've kept it. Who cares what she thinks? Oh, God; it's gone. That is the last straw.

What am I saying. What am I twittering on about. Pathos again, or is it bathos. I don't know what that means. Nor eclectic. Two words I'm always working into essays, hoping someone will tell me what they mean. I don't think Barnes knows, either.

Self-pitying, self-obsessed, self-indulgent, when it's Isabella who's had her life and her body shattered. She wasn't exactly at ease anyway, worried and tense, fearful of herself and the world. I thought I was doing my bit to calm her down, relax her. This will confirm her worst. They should be whipped, those two blokes, even hanged. No, I don't mean it. At least, I didn't mean it till now, now it's happened to someone I know and, er, let me see, let me think, someone I loved. There, I used that tired, old, beat-up, soppy word.

What a rotten nasty place the world is. It's not just in London: inner cities, inner dumps, high-rise squalor, the canker is everywhere. That's a Shakespearean sort of word I was planning to avoid. There I go again. Not even a straight run at simple, honest thoughts, without mucking it up with comments on the comments, remarks about the remarks. Why am I so self-conscious, why can't I be serious and sincere, at this time of all times, for Chrissake.

Is it me or the WP. Thinking thoughts keeps them abstract and ephemeral, and you can believe they are better and more profound than they are. Setting them down, you're forced to look at them, up on the big screen, or lying there in your secret diary, naked and clumsy, not quite what you meant, not quite what was in your mind, not at all polished and nowhere as brilliant as you had hoped. I s'pose most people feel like this, cleverer mentally than in speech, wiser in private than in public, clearer in the head than on the page, better with feelings than with actions. So when they are revealed, you're bound to hedge your bets, to mock and criticize if you don't want to appear a complete twat. To whom? Who's listening, who's looking, who's caring. Oh, I think I'll just give up. CANCEL everything.

How can it ever work now? She'll never trust me, despite the fact that I'm lovely. I'm one of them. She must think all men are sods.

How can she cope? How can I cope with her trying to cope? What a bloody mess. Whatever I do or say or try will be wrong. I'm not suited to the gentle, sensitive role. Bring on the clowns, the clumsy clots. Where will it lead. Months, if not years, of therapy. I can't wait, can't devote myself to all that.

Then what if someone else comes along into my life, who might have come along anyway, who might just have been waiting round the corner? Hello, Cart, what a long time you've taken, what kept you, you know I've been waiting just for you, kiss kiss kiss.

If that happens, how will I choose? I won't know if I'm dumping Isabella because of you-know-what, or if it was the natural end of that little road. I won't be able to do it, because I won't really know my motives or feelings or fears.

Either way, I'll feel terrible. I'm caught. I can't leave her, not now. Those hooligans have ruined my life as well. They should be shot.

She's saying I should go, and go now, because she, too, has thought it through. She's seen the rocks and stones ahead, even before I have. If I do go, saying it's her wish, her command, then it will be quick and clean and I can blame her.

But now I've realized that, I can't do it. I would be more of a pig, proving her right, doing it knowingly because I can't face the future. Too true, squire. I don't think I can, not that sort of bloody future. I'm scared.

But it shows she cares, is kind and wise and understands something of herself and us and what is likely to happen. A female sod, if there were such a person, would cling and weep and wail and really tie me down. So is that a hopeful sign?

Hmm, it could also be a sign of her over-sensitiveness. Someone so perceptive is going to see too far ahead too often and will always be aware and find it hard to forget and forgive and forgo. Sensitive souls can be neurotic. Passive people do have their place.

What if it's a complicated ruse? She knows what I'll think, and what I'll think of what she thinks, and then she'll think about what I'm thinking about, what I'm thinking she's thinking, like I'm doing now. Oh, just shurrup.

Oh, God, look at the time, what am I doing, wasting all this energy? Giving myself a headache, heartache, mindache, all that work to do, those exams, bloody hell. Do they matter now, potty bits of paper, compared with all these mortal body blows?

Two tall, dark strangers, two dominant people, have come into her life and ruined it.

Where the hell is my cloth? Just when I need it, need something, anything to hold on to.

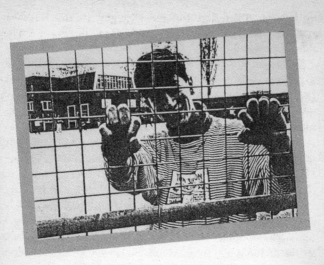

11 In Which Our Hero Receives His Final Reckoning

What a lovely Saturday morning, real summer at last, real birds on the wing, so what can these real plastic daffs be doing, scattered on the pavement? Some of our first-form apprentice vandals must have thrown them there. What is happening to the world, what is happening to standards, and what is going to happen to little me?

I'm trying awfully hard to be bright and cheerful. My heart with pleasure fills and dances with those dopey daffodils. Tum-ti-tum. How can a poet not be gay, in such a jocund compan-ay.

Even at the time (1807, if I remember correctly), that was really terrible, Willie, you should have tried again. I'm sure Mr Amstrad could have shown you the error of your ways, helped to reveal the full horror of your rotten rhymes. Thank

God I don't intend to study any of your lousy poetry. Not no more I don't.

I fear the worst, expect the least. Certain people who will this day learn their fate will find that it is merely bad, there will be those who will consider it fatal. On this bold St Crispin's morn. How did he creep in?

Has it got to be ever thus, the human condition pummelled and battered for such a piddling reason, made to compete and, therefore, forced to fail and be crucified? Right, I think that's the stage nicely set. You must know by now where this scene is set.

I got my O-level results through the post, weeks after they were all made public. That took the edge off the whole thing, softened the blow and got it in perspective, and I soon decided things weren't too bad anyway, considering that the examiners were obviously half-wits and did not recognize true genius. Or jokes.

This time, with A-levels, I stuck to the boringly expected, conventionally decreed answers and cut the smart remarks and witty comments. Let my ignorance be revealed, O wise ones. Why hide it. I had had, in fact, rather more important things on my mind, back in flaming June. I did think of writing something in the margins, please excuse, only this candidate has been under some pressures, only he's really good, go on, give him a B, the cheque's in the post.

Yup, and it did flame in June, doesn't it always. And there was also good European cup football on the telly, which I was forced to miss, well, parts of it, perhaps one or two of the action replays. At least it wasn't World Cup year. I wouldn't have done any work then.

It felt funny going into school on a Saturday morning anyway, but weirder in the middle of August when the playgrounds and classrooms are dead, buried with their memories. Old Barnes would soon arise and be twitting on the same old way, come September, with a new load of easily impressed suckers, soon to suss him out.

I could see a blackboard through the History-room window, one of the few still kept in classroom captivity. Ma Hoshkins always uses one as her only visual aid, ho ho, she'll be trotting that remark out, fresh as it never was, come September.

The Treaty of Versailles. Or was it the Six Chartists' Points? Or the reasons for the American Civil War? I couldn't quite see, as it was faded and dusty. God, what a load of cobblers, did I ever copy all those things down, did I really sit there at the back, trying to pretend I cared?

If I go on like this, I might get nostalgic, shedding a teeny tear; I might turn out to be the type of drip who drops back the next term, unable to keep away, looking for his roots or a place where he believed, for a while, he belonged. Or the sort who simply returns to show off that he's now a college cad, one of your actual 'students'. Or, if he's not an actual student, it's the fault of you buggers, you didn't help, so piss off all of you. There's usually one tortured loony who comes back to wreck the place. I looked forward to it. Always brightened up a new academic year.

Could that failure be me? I stopped to contemplate the world, to wonder why anyone should have plastic daffs in August and why anyone else would want to pinch them. A shortish pause on the campus, keeping myself pure and pre-A-level-results for just a moment longer. I'll be post-A-level-results for too long a time.

My heart was a-flutter. Not just through fear and consternation but also excitement and anticipation. God knows why, but I have been imagining in these last few weeks that maybe, might be, possibly, hell why not, rather than just scrape my three Bs, I might slide up and smash into the A

129

grades. Don't laugh. That's how I felt, it's a fact based on a fiction.

I could see the crowds round the front door, the main front door of the school, used only by staff and sixth-formers, big deal, what a privilege that is, and how thrilled I was, for half an hour at least. Should I battle to the front, or wait till they subsided? Would I have my misery to myself, or my jubilation?

I saw two girls in tears, one comforting the other, perhaps both had done badly, or one was sharing the other's misery. Girls do help each other at such times. Boys turn away. I didn't know either of them. How can they have been so hidden these last two years? Then I heard one moaning about Durham, it wasn't fair, she'd loved it so much, convinced it was going to happen, she'd already seen the room she wanted, decided the societies to join.

There was pushing and shoving, their bodies parted and out staggered Lol, all smiles, putting on a drunken lunge, clutching his head, falling down, getting up, making out he was knocked out, flattened by whatever news he'd got. With Lol it would be the same either way. He does have exams and life and other things in proportion. And either way, people would share in his result. Because he doesn't give a damn, so they wouldn't have to bother. There would be no need to show false emotions.

'Come on then,' I said. 'Stop messing around, what did you get?'

'Hold me!' he screamed. 'Kiss me! Hug me! You may even bonk me!'

'Okay, don't tell us then,' I said, pushing past him.

My eyes were dazzled by the sheets and sheets of computer print-out gibberish, none of which made sense, none of which seemed to list my subjects or my own sweet little name. I felt my mind going numb, my eyes disappearing, my brain cutting off. I felt faint.

There was a tug at my arm, then a violent yank and I was dragged out of the crowd and thrown on the ground.

'I did it!' Lol was yelling, standing over me. 'Three Cs. I'm a goddamn genius.'

'Great,' I said, getting up, feeling that his enthusiasm was now slightly obscene and not just unfunny.

Those results will be enough to get him somewhere for some degree course, yet he has not done any work whatsoever, while that poor Durham girl probably worked her heart out. What a lottery it all is, what a nonsense; surely by this stage in the millennium they could have created a better system without causing all this human chaos. It's an adults' trap to prepare us for the nasty, competitive world ahead of us, to make us compete, take it seriously, even begin to believe in it, so that the ones who do survive and succeed will, in turn, want it to continue. Otherwise they'll know it's all been a mockery, a waste of time. So it goes on.

Someone else pushed their way out of the crowd, staggering in high-heeled boots, stuck fast inside skin-tight jeans and wearing three tons of eye-shadow. How come a scrubber had got mixed up with all these brain-boxes?

It was Tracey, beaming, well chuffed, well pleased with her little self.

'I got them, Cartner,' she said, giving me a splodgy kiss and a little hug, looking over my shoulder for any better, chunkier shoulders.

'That's great, triffic, well done.'

I wondered what she'd got, touch of the clap perhaps, what a cheap nasty remark, and I'm supposed to be a reformed, repentant character, no more silly, hurtful comments. Okay then, perhaps she's got some GCSEs at last. The dreaded O-levels are no more. I was in the last batch. I saw service in the olden days, before the revolution. People will know my age for ever, once I mention O-levels.

'I'm going to the Royal Free,' she said, smirking.

My cheap nasty remark could be correct. Though maybe she's having an operation. Could it be a baby, even? Or just off for a quick one in a hospital shower. I've told everyone about them.

'I got the A-level I needed, Cartner. I'm going to be a nurse. You will come and let me practise on you, won't you? I have seen you naked, don't forget . . .'

I felt guilty and nasty while she smirked and winked and beamed and seemed about to reminisce rather too loudly about that night. Hold it, Trace, I thought, keep your voice down, there are certain people (who shall be nameless) whom I don't want to be told about that little incident. I started to move off.

'Hey, that's really good, Trace,' I said. 'I'll make a note to book into the Middlesex when I need my truss fixed.'

Clarrie almost walked straight into me, pulling herself from the throng, a set smile on her face. Resigned or relieved? I couldn't tell. Sloanes are taught from birth to have a tight upper headscarf, which gives nothing away. Like good Boy Scouts they can smile and whistle through most little local difficulties, oops, not an earthquake, oh, I say, what a bore.

She told me straight away. She'd ploughed. Made a pig's ear of it.

'No chance of Sussex now,' she said, sighing. 'Ah well, not to worry. On the old blower to Warwick, I suppose, Daddy knows someone there, probably all for the best. How did you do, Cartner? Jolly well, I'm sure.'

Wasn't that nice? No pretence. What a trooper. I gave her a hug. I must be getting soft in my old age. They say strange things do happen when you get to eighteen. I can feel a vote coming on.

'Actually, I don't know mine,' I said. 'Just about to find out, if I can.'

I got to the front of the crowds again, but still could make little sense of the sheets of results. I could distinguish some words this time, but they were names of subjects I did not know existed, names of people I had never heard of, and names of people I had heard of but didn't know they had other names. So that's how you spell his name, I thought. Good God, that's not her real name, is it? Perhaps his parents are not married. And that must be the stepfather's name. Blow me, Silas's first Christian name is Winston. How patriotic. I wonder if it was Churchill, or John Lennon. Remind me to ask him.

No need. He was standing beside me, looking solemn and serious, no hint either way of his results, scanning his eyes up and down all the sheets, memorizing every fact, every figure. Wish I had a photographic memory. Wish I had a memory.

'Straight to Cambridge then, Si,' I said. 'Got the old gown ordered.'

He didn't answer, still soaking up all the statistics.

'Did I ever tell you,' I said, 'that my dad got a Blue at Cambridge?'

'What?' said Silas.

'My dad,' I said. 'He would have got a Pink as well, but it was stuck behind the Black.'

'Ha, ha, bloody funny, and bloody old.'

'Well you can use it,' I said. 'Some of those public school prats you'll meet at Cambridge might not have heard it before.'

'I'm not going,' he said, bending down again, scooping up some scraps of Anthropology, the odds and sods of the Ancient History, Biology as a Foreign Language and Urdu for Beginners.

Oh, no, that must be the upset of the decade, like Spurs getting beaten by Dartmouth Park United's Sunday League Team. How awful. How could it have happened to Silas?

He's the most brilliant bloke in the school, and he worked like stink, knows it all backwards, even the double Maths paper he did on his own. Final proof, if final proof were needed, that examinations are a total nonsense. What chance have I, if the great Silas comes a cropper?

His name hit me in the eye, on the sheet before me, Double Maths. He'd got an A. His Physics was on the same sheet. Another A. Latin an A. English ditto. What was he talking about? He'd performed as predicted. Four As. As to spare, as Es would have been enough.

That Durham girl could have done with one of them: that was all she needed. There should be a system of sharing results out to the deserving. Such as me. I could open a swap shop, bring out your unwanted grades, your higher marks than you need. The examiners set these stupid rules, insisting on certain minimum grades, so why not take them at their word, slice off the unnecessary levels, pass them on to those who have fallen below and could usefully use them? If I'm unemployed and unoccupied next year, I could start an agency.

'I just applied to Cambridge in order to turn them down,' said Silas. 'You can't criticize something that you've failed yourself. I don't want any part of their elitist, racist, sexist entrance system. Anyway, the course at Manchester is better.'

So that's where he's going, along with Vinny. He scraped two Bs and a C, not quite the required offer, but he maintains they'll still take him.

'I'm having a year off, first,' said Vinny, 'to go round the world.' Quite a surprise. I thought Vinny had long since done the world. Going into orbit is about the only thing left for him to do.

Sally did brilliantly, so that was good, though I did expect it, after all her extra tutorials. Two As and a B. She's taking a year off, then trying Oxford. Silas is also going abroad, as he planned months ago. Home to Jamaica to spend a year with his grandparents.

I still couldn't find my own name. Have I become autodyslexic, a new disease fresh off the medical handbooks, word-blind to my own identity, or was I just scared to face it? I was shaking. The excitement had gone. All nerves now.

'Oh, you're still looking for your own,' said Silas. 'Three Bs, along with, let me see, twenty-three other people, including Armit, Ahmed, Dooms, Dineen, Edwards, Finkle, Gabrowski, three Patels . . .' He was running through them all, alphabetically, but I wasn't listening.

I'd done it. I was in. I was out. I would be up and away, off to pastures new, people unknown, places still novel. I'm not taking a year off. Certainly not. I want the next stage to begin now, to leave the family nest and start flying, not putting it off. Wheeeee.

I waited till Silas had gone, his little curly head jampacked with names and numbers. I wanted to check, to see it in writing, just in case he might have made a teensy-weensy mistake – hardly possible with him, but he must be human, deep down somewhere. I was thinking only of a microscopic error, let's say a small 'A' instead of a B, lower case would do, in, say, English. After all that work I did, all those brilliant essays, plus my natural talents.

He was correct. What optimism to hope for something better, what conceit to expect it. Eight months ago, at Christmas, I would have given a Queen's ransom to know that those three Bs were in the bag, or a week's wages on the old ice-cream scoops. Must keep things in proportion. They're only exams, only skittery bits of paper. There are far more important things in heaven or life, Dear Brutus, than one can ever dream of. Now the dream will be coming true, this very September, as I live and breathe and have my own data disc.

'Hi, I've heard,' she said, giving me a kiss. 'Well done.'

I was coming out of the school gates, still in a stupor, and bumped right into her.

Oh, no, I'd forgotten to look at her results. The new, wonderful, caring, unselfish me. Not much of a new leaf. Not much of a helpmate, soul mate, sensitive kindred spirit sort of mate. Did Silas mention her name? I should have been concentrating.

'It's good we both got the same,' she said, taking my arm, walking away from school together. 'Sort of neat.'

'Sort of apt,' I said.

'Sort of creepy,' she said.

'As we are going to Sussex together,' I said, 'might as well start off in step. Never know how we might end up.'

'Cold, probably,' she said.

'Oh, no, won't be cold, not no more we won't,' I said.

After the greyness of the last two months, the hard times, the slow times, then the hesitant, careful times, then the nearly good times, knuckling down to work times, conquering it together times, talking it through times, we made it. But you don't want to hear all that. Do you?

I know we've been through the thins and thicks together, WP, my old mate, my friend in times of grief, but I decided to spare you the last two months. I was too busy living it and working at it to tell you about it, so that's a good sign. I had someone else to talk to, a real kindred spirit at last, which is what we all want in life, hey ho. Anyway, you're clever, you're smart, you can guess what it's been like. Oh, forgot, you can't guess. No imagination. You need to be programmed, like so many other poor sods out there. Well that's you finished.

'I predict it will be hot from now on,' I said. 'With, of course, occasional spells of cold, got to expect that, perhaps a few showers, dull periods, patches of cloud in the afternoons, but mainly it will be bright, with lots and lots of hots.'

'Your place or mine?'

'I think this calls for a shower at the Royal Free,' I said.

'Or our first whole weekend in Brighton,' she said.

'Right, I'll go home and pack my things.'

No one was in when I got home, which was lucky, but on the hall floor, right in the middle so that even I couldn't miss it, was a pile of rather scruffy photocopied sheets and a scribbled note from my mum.

Hope you like the photies. I had to do them for my evening-class project, which was to do someone who didn't want to be photographed and didn't know they were being done! Now who could that be! They are the best in the class, so Sir says, and the originals are now on show at the Institute! I knew you would be pleased for me and would like copies. Good job you never saw me in Brighton! Or McDonalds! Or outside the Royal Free! Your loving Mother.

What a pain parents can be. How embarrassing. Why does she use all these exclamation marks?

And as for her crummy snaps, remind me not to go anywhere near that stupid Institute.

I ran upstairs, looking at the copies. Some of them are a bit blurry. Not bad, I suppose, for a beginner. These classes do keep them off the gin and the Valium, so one should not scoff. Perhaps I can use them.

When I got into my room to start packing, I noticed at once that the WP was on, flickering away in the corner. I must have left it like that, which was stupid. I really think my memory is going.

Then I realized there was a message on it, glimmering and shimmering, winking almost, as if for once there was a smile on the face of my friendly old Wee Pee.

DEAR CARTNER, YOU FORGOT I COULD USE THE WP, YOU FOOL. BEEN READING YOUR RUBBISH FOR MONTHS, WHEN I'VE BEEN REALLY BORED, OR MY ENORMOUS UGLY FRIENDS WITH THEIR HORRIBLE THIGHS HAVE NOT BEEN AROUND. YOU PIG. BUT I GOT MY OWN BACK EVERY TIME YOU WERE NASTY ABOUT MY MUSIC, MY VOICE, MY LAUGHING, MY THICK SKIN, MY COOKING, MY ENORMOUS BODY, BEING A PEASANT, SPOILED, A SLUT, MEAN, FAT, LAZY. LOOK BACK AND YOU'LL SEE WHAT HAPPENED EVERY TIME YOU WERE NASTY TO ME. I GOT YOU, BUM FACE, AND IT SERVED YOU RIGHT. THE ONLY THING I AGREED WITH WAS ABOUT YOU. VERY SELF-CONSCIOUS, SELF-INDULGENT, WHAT A PHONEY YOU CAN BE, BUT YOU WERE ONLY SEVENTEEN AND THREE QUARTERS AT THE TIME, SO I'LL LET YOU OFF. BUT I WAS FURIOUS, YOU SOD. I WAS GOING TO TELL THE WRINKLIES, OR BLACKMAIL YOU, BUT INSTEAD I GOT MY OWN BACK IN MY OWN LITTLE WAYS. SORRY ABOUT THAT. I DID READ WHAT HAPPENED WITH MARIE, BEFORE YOU WIPED IT OFF, BUT YOU CAN TRUST ME, AND ALSO YOUR LETTER TO ISABELLA, YOU HALF-WIT, YOU NEARLY BLEW IT THERE. ANYWAY, HERE'S YOUR HORRIBLE TRAINERS. THEY'VE BEEN STINKING OUT MY ROOM. YOU'LL FIND YOUR PRECIOUS PARKER PEN ON THE LAVATORY SHELF. THOSE BORING SPURS PROGRAMMES ARE IN THE CUPBOARD UNDER THE STAIRS. I PUT THE BOXER SHORTS IN THE DUSTBIN. AND IT WAS ME WHO RANG DIM. SORRY ABOUT THAT AS WELL. DIDN'T THINK HE'D ACTUALLY SACK YOU.

P.S. IF YOU REALLY WANT YOUR COMFORT CLOTH BACK, LOOK IN THE AMSTRAD MANUAL. I KNEW FROM THIS MESS YOU CAN'T HAVE BEEN USING IT. KEEP IN TOUCH. GOOD LUCK NEXT YEAR. YOUR FRIEND, SISTER SEZ, WHO SAYS ENTER AND EXIT AND FINALLY END · · ·